THE SECRET CIPHER

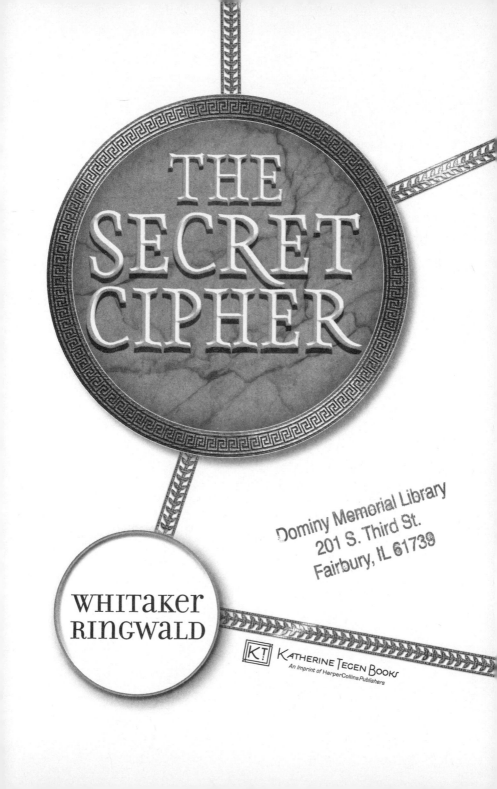

THE SECRET CIPHER

WHITAKER RINGWALD

KATHERINE TEGEN BOOKS
An Imprint of HarperCollins Publishers

Katherine Tegen Books is an imprint of HarperCollins Publishers.

The Secret Cipher
Copyright © 2015 by HarperCollins Publishers
All rights reserved. Printed in the United States of America.
No part of this book may be used or reproduced in any manner
whatsoever without written permission except in the case of brief
quotations embodied in critical articles and reviews. For information
address HarperCollins Children's Books,
a division of HarperCollins Publishers, 195 Broadway,
New York, NY 10007.
www.harpercollinschildrens.com
ISBN 978-0-06-221617-5
Typography by Carla Weise
15 16 17 18 19   CG/RRDH   10 9 8 7 6 5 4 3 2 1
❖

First Edition

For cryptographers everywhere

1
ETHAN

FACT: *I am thirteen years old and I feel like I've already lived two lives—the one before the magical Greek urn, and the one after.*

It's still hard for me to use the word *magical*. Until one month ago, I would have bet my life on the fact that magic doesn't exist.

Yesterday, CNN ran a story about a kid who'd been born blind, but when he turned sixteen, he got a double cornea transplant. It was an experimental procedure. When he opened his eyes after surgery and saw light and shapes for the very first time, he kinda freaked.

That's how it feels to me when I lie in bed at night and remember the afternoon in the Thomas Jefferson Memorial when my cousin, Jax, opened the Greek urn and magic burst out. I'd been blind to the truth, but now I've seen it.

Maybe "freaked" isn't a strong enough word.

Before Jax opened the urn, the world was a normal place full of things that can be proven. Buoyancy causes objects to float, gravity keeps our feet on the ground, evaporation makes puddles disappear. Earthquakes and volcanoes are caused by the shifting of tectonic plates and thunder occurs during the cooling of superheated air. These are the laws I'd learned—laws based on reason and logic, cause and effect. Tides are predictable. Time moves at a steady pace. Science rules.

Or maybe I should say, *ruled*.

Before Jax opened the urn, there were stories about gods. I never paid much attention to these stories. Zeus and his thunderbolt, Poseidon and his trident, Hades and his underworld of lost souls. These were myths, pure entertainment, written thousands of years ago by people who were trying to explain things that seemed totally unexplainable. These stories were as fantastical as *Grimms' Fairy Tales*. Who

2

would ever believe that a big bad wolf could dress up like someone's grandmother and say, "The better to eat you with, my dear"? Likewise, who would believe that a pantheon of gods could live on an invisible mountain and stuff human emotions, like hope, faith, and love, into clay urns?

You can't pack emotions into containers. They're not peanut butter sandwiches. They're *feelings*.

"Hey, pass the ketchup, will ya?"

Jax stared at me from across the restaurant table. A few strands of frizzy black hair hung in her eyes. The rest of her hair was pulled into a ponytail, as usual.

"Hello?" She tapped her fork on her plate. "I'm starvin' over here."

"Uh, sorry." I grabbed the bottle and handed it to her. I don't use public ketchup bottles. I read an article about the variety of germs that live on the mouth of the bottle, right where the ketchup comes out. It's disgusting. But I didn't share this information. Jax didn't care about germs. She used public drinking fountains all the time. And I've seen her eat a chicken strip after she'd dropped it on the sidewalk.

"Thanks." She squirted a thick line down the

3

middle of her huevos rancheros. Ever since she learned that she was half Latina, a fact that had been kept from her all her life, she'd been ordering a lot of Mexican food. She dug into the eggs as if she hadn't eaten in days. "Don't you like your food?" she asked.

"It's good," I said. Melted butter dripped down the sides of my short stack. I ignored the public syrup bottle and took a bite. I wasn't feeling very hungry. My sinuses were inflamed, thanks to the record-level of pollen in the air.

We were sitting in the Chatham Diner, the best place for breakfast in Chatham, New Jersey. We didn't have to pay for our breakfast because Jax's mom, my aunt Lindsay, worked there as a waitress. Jax had woken me up early and we'd ridden our bikes to the diner. She never slept in because, according to Jax's philosophy, sleep is a waste of time. My dad, who has a master's degree in chemistry, says Jax has a lot of fast-twitch muscles, and that's why it's hard for her to sit still and why she's always running everywhere. Mom, who has a master's degree in psychology, says Jax is hyperactive and should avoid caffeine and sugar. Tyler, my older brother, says Jax is a super spaz.

The things he calls me are way worse.

"I'm so totally bored," Jax said, her mouth crammed with eggs and tortilla. "What are we going to do today?"

I could think of lots of things to do. The new issue of *Science Monthly* had come in yesterday's mail. And a couple days ago, I'd checked out a stack of books from the library. But reading was something to do alone, and Jax had been super clingy lately. I couldn't blame her. The urn experience had been terrifying.

To make a long story short, here's what happened. One month ago, on her twelfth birthday, Jax got a strange metal box in the mail. It was sent by our great-aunt Juniper Vandegrift, a relative we'd never heard of. The box wouldn't open but a message appeared on an LED screen that was set into its lid. It was a riddle. The box would open only at a precise, predetermined spot. So, with Tyler's help and some geometry, we found the right spot in Washington, DC. But we nearly got killed in the process.

It turned out Great-Aunt Juniper was an archaeologist who'd discovered an ancient Greek artifact—a clay urn. But this wasn't a typical clay pot that you'd find sitting in a museum. This one held a dangerous power.

Way back in the beginning of time, Zeus made

three urns and gave them to a girl named Pyrrha. One urn contained Love, one contained Faith, and the third held Hope. If Pyrrha felt sad, she could open whichever urn she chose and be filled with that emotion. Imagine if you could fill miniature urns with love, faith, and hope and sell them on the internet or one of those shopping channels. They'd be an instant cure for depression, dark thoughts, and doubt. I'm guessing that would make you one of the richest people in the world.

But after Zeus gave Pyrrha her special gifts, Pyrrha's father, Epimetheus, went insane with jealousy. He felt that the gods had ignored him, for they'd never given him anything special. So he stole the urns, planning on keeping Love, Faith, and Hope for himself. But when he opened the urns, the contents were destroyed by his evil nature. Now empty, the urns seemed useless, so Epimetheus buried them, trying to hide the evidence.

Time passed and eventually the Greek gods disappeared from the human world. The urns lay untouched, buried by centuries of dirt and debris. Then, during an archaeological dig on the Greek island of Kassos, Great-Aunt Juniper dug up one of them— the urn of Hope. Curious about what it contained, she uncorked it. A tornado shot out of the clay jar and swirled around the site. Juniper watched with confusion as every member of the excavation team collapsed, except for her. After swirling around each of the victims, the wind calmed and disappeared back inside the urn.

During all that time underground, the urn had transformed. Because it had been created for one purpose—to hold Hope—it had begun to *crave* hope. Literally. So when our great-aunt opened it, it sucked hope from everyone it could reach. Only Juniper was safe because she'd been holding the urn at the time.

Ever see someone who's had hope sucked from his soul? I have. When we were at the Thomas Jefferson Memorial, Tyler was attacked by the urn. He ended up in the hospital. It was the worst day of our lives.

"Hey." Jax's mom stood at the end of the table, a pot of coffee in her hand. "How are your pancakes?"

"Great," I said, making sure to look right into my aunt's eyes. My counselor always reminded me to do that.

The customer in the next booth held up his mug. Aunt Lindsay filled it, then turned back to our table. "So, do you two have big plans today?" The question had a suspicious tone. Who could blame her? Jax and I had gotten into more than our share of trouble lately.

"Not really," I said. Jax groaned. What had I done?

"No plans?" Aunt Lindsay smiled. "Well, that means you have time to do some chores. The backyard needs to be mowed and the walkway is full of weeds. That should keep you busy." A bell chimed from behind the counter.

"Order up," Michael called. He was the morning cook.

As soon as Aunt Lindsay had walked away, Jax leaned over her plate and narrowed her eyes. "Thanks a lot," she said. "Now we're stuck working all day."

"Sorry," I said. But I didn't mind helping my aunt. She was a single parent and never had enough money to hire a gardener. My parents had a whole team of guys who came once a week to mow the lawn, weed the beds, and clean the pool. "I can do most of it. You don't have to."

Jax sighed. "I guess it's better than sitting around waiting. Do you think we'll hear from Juniper today?" It was the same question she'd asked every day for the last month.

I shrugged. "I don't know." After the incident in the Jefferson Memorial, Great-Aunt Juniper had disappeared, taking the urn of Hope with her. She'd told us she was going to find a way to destroy it. That would be the best thing to do. If the urn fell into the wrong hands, it could be used as a weapon. "It's possible we might never hear from her again," I told Jax.

"I hate not knowing," Jax said.

I stared out the window. Usually I would have said that I also hate not knowing. I'm the kid who loves facts and information. But during the last month, I'd woken up every morning wishing I'd never seen the urn's powers.

For the first time in my life, I didn't want to *know*.

2
JAX

"I'm melting," I complained.

"The news predicted a high of ninety-two," Ethan said after blowing his nose. "Ten degrees hotter than last year."

We were in my small backyard. Ethan had mowed the grass. The mower's blades had stirred dandelion pollen into the air so he was having a huge allergy attack. How many times in a row can a person sneeze before his head explodes? Seriously. Good thing he always had a bunch of tissues stuffed in his pockets.

I tossed weeds into a bucket. Yard work was the last thing I wanted to do, and to make it even worse, my mom didn't pay for chores.

"I'm hot too," Ethan said.

"Take off your shirt," I told him. Boys are lucky that way. They can strip down to their boxers and no one cares.

"But I don't have sunblock."

I didn't have any either. I rarely used the stuff. My skin's tan like coffee, while Ethan's is as pale as a fish belly. While I've got black hair, his is brown, but you never see it because he wears a baseball cap most of the time. He likes to hide under its brim. He's übershy.

I pulled another dandelion. Its roots were super stubborn, as if it knew I was coming to get it. "I . . . hate . . . pulling . . . weeds," I groaned as I yanked it from the ground. My buttcrack was starting to get sweaty. "Forget this," I said, peeling off the gardening gloves. Then I hurried into the garage, looking for something that would make us both feel better.

There it was, behind a stack of snow tires—my old Hello Kitty swimming pool.

"Turn on the hose," I told Ethan as I dragged the plastic pool onto the grass.

"Why don't we go swim in my pool?" he asked. A few years ago, his parents had installed a pool with a deep end and a diving board. It was super nice but I didn't feel like riding all the way over there. I set the hose inside.

"This'll work just fine." I sat in the pool in my shorts and T-shirt, my legs hanging over the edge. "Ahhhhh," I said, as the water poured in. "That's better."

July is the worst time to be stuck in Chatham. The humidity makes everything wilt. Mom and I usually went camping by the lake, but she was working extra hours at the diner, so I was stuck. Other than our bikes, the only way to get around was to beg my older cousin, Tyler, to drive us. But ever since our trip to Washington, DC, he'd been holed up in his room, *recovering*.

"You know, I've been thinking," I said. Water began to spill over the top of the pool, so Ethan turned off the hose. "If Juniper hadn't disappeared, we could have become really famous. I mean, we have proof that the Greek gods existed."

"*Had* proof," he corrected. "We don't have the urn anymore."

I'd spent a lot of time thinking about what might have happened. "We could have been on magazine covers and morning talk shows. We could have gotten a million-dollar book deal." I smiled dream-ily. With that much money, I'd build my own pool with a diving board and deep end. "They'd make a movie about us. They'd call it *The Secret Box Adventure*. We'd have a red-carpet premiere and wear gowns. Well, I'd wear a gown."

Ethan didn't smile back. It was easy for me to read his thoughts. We'd spent so much time together, I could practically see inside his brain. *Jax spends too much time imagining things. She makes up too many stories, like the ones where she pretends that her father is an astronaut or a rock star.*

"They can't make a movie about us because we can't tell anyone about the urn," he said.

Ethan, Tyler, and I had agreed on the following fact: if the world knew about the urn's power, then we'd all be in danger. Someone would ultimately use it for evil. There is no positive reason to suck hope from a person's soul.

I sighed. The imaginary opening credits to my movie faded before my eyes like smoke. "I know it's a secret. You don't need to remind me."

Ethan sat on the grass and took off his black Converse sneakers. Then he dangled his feet in the plastic pool. I splashed water on my face. "How hot do you think it is in Hades?"

"Hades?" Ethan held back a sneeze.

"Yeah. The Greek underworld. It's their version of hell. I've been reading about it." Usually I read travel guides. They're my favorite books. But I went to the public library and got this book about Greek mythology so I could understand more about what had happened to us. "How hot do you think it is down there?"

"What do you mean *is*?" he asked. "The Greek gods are gone. So if they're gone, then their underworld must be gone too." He was always trying to be logical.

"Okay, fine." I flicked water at him. "How hot do you think it *was* in Hades?"

Ethan thought for a moment. He was super good at collecting facts. "Well, Death Valley is the hottest place on earth. Its record temperature is one hundred thirty-four degrees. The surface of the sun is somewhere around ten thousand degrees Fahrenheit. So I'm going to guess that Hades is between those two." Then he shook his head. "I can't believe we're having this conversation."

Until a month ago, Ethan would have said there was no such place as Hades. He would have told me to go talk to Tyler. Tyler's obsessed with Greek and Roman mythology. He designed a multiplayer combat game called Cyclopsville, where the players search ancient ruins and fight mythological beasts. I have to admit that the exploding cyclops heads are pretty cool.

Even though my butt was going numb from the cold, I sank lower into the water. My thoughts turned to our great-aunt, who'd taken us on this amazing adventure, and then disappeared. Since then, the only message we'd gotten from her was a single email that I'd opened on my computer.

TO: Jacqueline Malone
FROM: Juniper
SUBJECT: How Are You?

But there'd been nothing in the email—no message, no photographs. Zero!

"I think Juniper's being rude," I grumbled. "We saved her from kidnappers. She should at least give us a call. We deserve to know what's going on."

"I'm glad she hasn't called," Ethan said.

Maybe he was right. Because of our great-aunt, Tyler, Ethan, and I had almost been killed by a pair of international felons named Martha and George Camel. They'd kidnapped Juniper. Then they'd chased us through Washington, DC. Mr. Camel had pointed a gun at Tyler's head, and Mrs. Camel pointed a gun at Ethan and me!

"It would definitely make a good movie," I said. "And if we had more adventures, there'd be a sequel."

"A sequel?" Ethan sneezed. "Are you serious? A sequel has to be even more exciting than the first movie. That would mean something even worse would have to happen."

I sat up real straight. "What if something even worse *already* happened? What if Juniper's been kidnapped again and that's why we haven't heard from her?"

"The Camels are in prison," Ethan said. "Besides, there's no reason to think Juniper's been hurt. She's probably too busy to call."

I fidgeted. I hate waiting for anything. I always open the microwave before the popcorn is fully popped. And I refuse to get milk shakes at Pete's Soda Fountain because they take too long making them by hand. So waiting a whole month for a message was driving me crazy. "But what if she's in trouble and that's why she hasn't called? What if—"

A phone rang. We both turned around and stared at my house. Mom still kept a landline in the kitchen. It rang again.

I grabbed the edge of the pool. "Do you think . . . ?" Water splashed over the sides as I scrambled out. "Please be Juniper, please be Juniper," I chanted as I ran across the freshly mowed grass. After flinging open the kitchen door, I hurried inside, reaching the phone on the fourth ring. "Hello?"

"Hello," a woman said.

I sighed. The voice didn't belong to Juniper. Once again, total disappointment. I was ready to hang up, because that's the best way to deal with a sales call, when the voice said, "I'm not sure if I have the right number, but there is an elderly woman in our care and we found this phone number written inside her bandana."

3
ETHAN

FACT: *The immune system is supposed to stand guard and protect against dangerous invaders, like the bird flu and the bubonic plague. But sometimes it overreacts to things that aren't dangerous, like tree pollen and cat fur. The result— itchy eyes, sneezing, and inflamed sinuses, which is what always happens to me at the beginning of summer. I'm an immune system mess.*

Oh, and then there are the stress-induced nosebleeds. I've been getting those all my life. Jax never makes fun of me, but Tyler always does. He calls me an inferior life form.

Me and my allergies waited by the pool while Jax answered the phone. It was probably a sales call. But what were the odds that it was our great-aunt? If I wanted to calculate the actual number, I'd have to ask Tyler, captain of the high school's Math Olympiad team.

"Ethan!" Jax frantically waved at me from the doorway, the phone cord stretched tight. Then she disappeared back into the kitchen.

Uh-oh.

Jax's house had no air-conditioning, so the kitchen felt stuffy. Fruit flies fluttered around a pair of overripe bananas and a pile of dirty dishes filled the sink. Jax stood at the counter, the phone pressed to her ear. Water dripped off her shorts and pooled around her bare feet. I wiped my feet on the mat, leaving behind a bunch of grass blades. "What's going on?"

Jax pressed the phone's speaker button. The voice on the other end was female. She was in the middle of an explanation. "The Sisters of Mercy treats elderly patients suffering from dementia and memory loss. This particular patient was found at the Museum of Fine Arts in Boston. She couldn't remember who she was or how she'd gotten to the museum. Massachusetts

General Hospital treated her and diagnosed her with having suffered a cerebrovascular accident."

"A what?" Jax asked.

"A stroke, which means that the blood supply to her brain was cut off for a short period of time, causing damage." The woman cleared her throat. "She was brought to Sisters of Mercy a few days ago but we still don't know who she is. She has no identification and no family member has claimed her. We're calling her Jane Doe. As I said, your phone number was written inside her bandana."

Jax and I shared a look. The last time we saw Juniper, she'd been wearing a bandana.

The woman continued. "She's elderly, probably in her eighties. And she has long white hair. It was in a braid when they found her."

"Braids and a bandana?" I said. "That sounds like—"

Jax grabbed my arm, silencing me with a squeeze. "Don't say anything yet," she whispered. "We don't know what's going on."

"So?" the woman asked. "Does she sound familiar?"

Jax pursed her lips together and tapped her fingers on the counter. "I might know her," she said cautiously. "She sounds like a lady who lived down the street."

Jax was protecting our great-aunt. For many years, Juniper had been hiding from the world. She'd had herself "erased" from the internet. She'd come to us only because she'd needed help. So until we knew the whole story, we'd continue to keep her secrets.

"Can we talk to her?" Jax asked.

"I'm afraid Jane Doe is not allowed to make calls right now. The police are here and . . ." She paused.

"Why are the police there?" I asked.

"It's complicated. Will you come and see if you know her? It's important that we contact her next of kin. We are the Sisters of Mercy Convalescent Center, in Boston."

"Okay." Jax grabbed a pad of paper and pencil and wrote down the address. "Thank you. We'll be there as soon as we can." Then she hung up.

"I hope Juniper's okay," I said, remembering our neighbor Mrs. Purcell, who'd suffered a massive stroke. It had left her paralyzed and unable to speak. One year had passed and Mrs. Purcell still couldn't walk.

"Juniper's faking," Jax said with total certainty. "I just know it. Something happened and she needed a place to hide. What better place than a hospital where no one knows you?" She hurried from the kitchen.

"Uh . . . you can't fake a stroke," I pointed out. "They would have done a CAT scan on her brain. Where are you going?"

"I'm gonna change into some dry clothes. We've got to figure out how to get to Boston."

A knot formed in my stomach. I was happy that we hadn't heard from our great-aunt. It was nice not being chased by villains. It was nice not carrying around an urn that could suck hope from people's souls. I'd been looking forward to a predictable summer without any more Greek god activity. But Jax wanted to jump right back in while I wanted to go back outside and rake grass.

Fact: Each of us shares about 99.5 percent of our DNA with everyone else on the planet. And if you're closely related, like a brother or a cousin, then you share even more.

So why were Jax and I so different?

I'm not an adventurous person. I'm happy to read and observe. I'll probably go into some kind of research, like my dad. Test tubes don't look at you weirdly when you try to say something appropriate but it comes out as a list of facts.

I walked out of the kitchen, then stood at the bottom of the stairs. Jax's bedroom was on the second floor. "I want to point out that we are forbidden to have anything to do with our great-aunt," I hollered. "If our parents find out that we met her, we're gonna get grounded or worse."

We weren't supposed to know Great-Aunt Juniper because she'd been shunned by our parents. Before Jax was born, Aunt Lindsay had gone to visit Juniper, who'd been working in Washington, DC, for the International Society of Archaeologists. During the visit, Aunt Lindsay fell in love with a man who was working as Juniper's intern. Aunt Lindsay got pregnant with Jax, and Lindsay and the man were going to get married but he disappeared. He didn't leave a note or an address. Jax was raised not knowing anything about her father.

But last month, when we met Juniper for the first time, she confessed that the man hadn't been an intern. He was actually a professional thief and an expert on breaking codes. He'd been hired by the society to retrieve a stolen artifact. He'd gone into hiding and Juniper couldn't reveal his whereabouts. Aunt Lindsay had felt betrayed. She'd said Juniper should have warned her not to get involved with this man. She'd told Juniper to never contact our family again.

I think Aunt Lindsay was embarrassed that she'd fallen in love with a criminal. She'd trusted him and he'd abandoned her and her baby. She didn't want Jax to know the truth, so it was easier to blame everything on Juniper. That's why Jax grew up without a father and why we never knew about our great-aunt.

"Jax?" I called. "Are you listening to me? Boston is almost two hundred and fifty miles away and neither of us is old enough to drive."

"I don't care if Boston is a million miles away. We have to get there." She raced down the stairs in new, dry clothes. Then she grabbed my cell phone. "I'm calling Tyler." She bounced on her toes while the phone rang. Tyler's voice boomed from the speaker.

"If you're calling the New Jersey Math Olympiad champion and the co-creator of the mind-blowing game Cyclopsville, then you've reached the right number. Unfortunately for *you*, I'm currently engaged in activities that your puny mind cannot comprehend, so leave a message, dude." *Beep.*

Jax groaned and hung up. "Where is he?"

I checked my watch. "He's at the comic-book store. There's a tournament today."

Her mouth fell open. "He left the house? Really?"

24

It wasn't unusual for Tyler to stay in his bedroom all day during the summer, working on his computer. Jax often joked about him being a vampire who couldn't be exposed to daylight. But for the last month, he'd stayed in his room because he'd been too depressed to go anywhere. There'd been a whole week when he could barely get out of bed. Apparently that's what happens when hope is sucked from your soul.

I will never forget the scene. When Mr. and Mrs. Camel drew guns on us, there'd been only one way to disarm them. The plan was for Jax to open the urn. We'd be safe from the effects as long as we were touching the urn's surface—it protects those who hold it. But Tyler had been standing on the other side of the memorial, with a gun to his back. In a moment of unbelievable courage, he ordered Jax to open the urn. He sacrificed himself so that the Camels could be caught. When the urn unleashed its tornado and sucked hope from Mr. and Mrs. Camel and an unlucky security guard, it also sucked hope from Tyler.

After Jax corked the urn, we rushed to Tyler's side. He lay like a limp noodle, his eyes wide open, staring at nothing. He couldn't talk. He couldn't move. Mr. and Mrs. Camel and the security guard were in the same condition. I called 911. As ambulance sirens wailed, Juniper disappeared, taking the urn with her.

By the time our parents arrived at the hospital in DC, the doctors had no idea what was wrong, so they said it was a viral infection. Viruses can spread fast, so it was possible that the Camels and the security guard had all come down with it. Of course they didn't suspect a Greek urn had been the cause of everyone's weird symptoms. Who would?

Once they came out of their trances, Mr. and Mrs. Camel were shipped back to England, where they were wanted on forgery charges. The security guard went home with his family and Tyler spent the next four weeks recovering in his room. And he hadn't left the house until today.

"Let's go," Jax said, handing my phone back.

"Uh . . ." I stalled. "We haven't finished weeding. And I was thinking about sharpening the mower's blades."

She folded her arms. "Ethan, you can come up with a million excuses but you're not going to talk me out of this."

"It would be impossible for me to come up with *a million* excuses," I told her.

She smiled. "Impossible? Do you still believe things are *impossible?*"

"Yes," I said, trying to sound certain. I would cling to denial as long as I could . . . like a germ clinging to the side of a public ketchup bottle.

4

JAX

The heat wasn't going to keep me from riding extra fast. I took the lead. Even if Ethan had wanted to be in front, he wouldn't have been able to outpedal me. I was like a bullet.

When we got to Merlin's Comics, sweat coated the backs of my knees and Ethan could barely catch his breath. We locked our bikes in the rack, then went inside.

I'd grown up in Chatham, but I'd only been inside this store a few times. Comic books weren't my thing. The place was cluttered with displays of memorabilia and collectibles. Board games were stacked on shelves. T-shirts and costumes hung from racks. A table of comic-book bins sat in the center of the room. It was Geek Central.

"Pee-ew," I said, scrunching my face. It smelled just like Tyler's bedroom. If someone bottled that stench it would be called *Eau de Gamer*.

Ethan winced. He wasn't anything like his older brother. Ethan was a full-fledged nerd, which is totally different from being a gamer. Ethan was socially awkward and liked to read all the time. But he also liked to take showers. And he wore deodorant and changed his socks. Tyler and his weirdo friends thought personal hygiene was a waste of time. They had scruffy beards, uncombed hair, and armpit stains. When Tyler complained about not having a girlfriend, Aunt Cathy told him that girls don't like guys who stink and she threatened to run him through a car wash. Uncle Phil said that Tyler would one day meet a girl who would appreciate him, regardless of his body odor. I'm not so sure that's true.

"Do you see him?" I asked, standing on my tip-toes.

"Over there." Ethan pointed.

I walked around a large inflatable dragon and headed toward the back room while Ethan stayed by the door. There were about forty people crammed into the small space. That's not quite a crowd but it's definitely a group. For Ethan, groups were worse than crowds because he couldn't hide as easily. I spotted a couple of girls in the store, but they were as rare as the green clovers in a box of Lucky Charms.

"Hey, Tyler," I called, cupping my hands around my mouth.

A huge guy stepped in front of me. "The gaming cave is currently off-limits, my lady."

My lady? I looked up. Whoa! He must have been seven feet tall. His nametag read *Merlin*, so I guessed he was the owner. "I need to talk to my cousin."

"Interruptions are prohibited during play." His Batman T-shirt stretched over his enormous gut. He'd braided his long beard so he looked like he'd just stepped out of *Lord of the Rings*. "You'll have to wait until the end of the round."

"Are you serious?" I asked.

"As serious as Venser sacrificing his heart for Karn. This is a Magic tournament."

"You mean, tricks and stuff?"

"Tricks and stuff? Not *that* kind of magic." He

started talking to me the way Tyler often did, as if I was a complete idiot and he was teaching me something I should already know. "Magic: The Gathering is a two-or-more-player game composed of trading cards. Each round is a battle between Planeswalkers, using spells, items, and creatures."

"Are you telling me it's a stupid card game?"

"I beg your pardon?" Merlin raised his unibrow. "Stupid card game?" Some of the players had turned and were staring me. "I'll have you know that over twelve million people worldwide are Magic: The Gathering enthusiasts."

"So what? It's still a *card* game." Maybe I sounded a bit rude, but seriously, he was worried about a game and I was worried about my great-aunt and an urn that could turn people into zombies. When I tried to step around him, he blocked my path. Normally I would have complained to the manager, but this guy owned the place. I sighed. "Fine, I'll wait. How long will it take?"

"Until someone has won." Merlin pointed to a couch by the cash register. "You're welcome to sit, my lady."

"The name is Jax." I stomped over and slumped onto the couch. Ethan joined me. "So this is the reason Tyler left his room? For a Magic game? I don't get it."

Ethan pointed at a trophy that sat next to the cash register.

"Oh. Right." Nothing more needed to be said. My cousin Tyler went after trophies the way a shark goes after blood. His collection was on display in his family's den, complete with custom-made shelving and special gallery-style lighting.

I squirmed. Then squirmed some more. If I sat up real straight and craned my neck to the left, I could barely see Tyler. He hadn't noticed us or maybe he was ignoring us. "I overload my Mizzium Mortars," he announced to his opponent, who looked about ten years old.

"Crud!" the kid cried, sliding a bunch of cards to the side. "My graveyard's getting full."

"Guess all those expensive cards your parents bought you were a waste of money," Tyler said with a snicker. "Your time would have been better spent sitting in your room waiting for puberty. I'm last year's champion, in case you didn't know. Prepare to be humiliated."

No doubt about it, Tyler was back to normal. A few weeks ago, I wasn't sure he'd recover. I'd been sitting in his room and I'd asked him what it had been like to have hope sucked from his soul. He said it was the darkest feeling he'd ever had. He'd felt cold inside, like he was made of ice.

For the last three years, a sign had been posted on Tyler's bedroom door: *Embrace the Zombie Apocalypse.* He took it down after he got home from the hospital. He said it felt too real.

A cheer arose from the game cave. I whispered in Ethan's ear. "If you distract the Merlin dude, then I can sneak behind the dragon and get to Tyler."

"Distract him?"

"Yeah. Pretend you're having an allergy attack and you can't breathe. Pretend you need an EpiPen." I nudged his arm. "Please?"

"But what if he has an EpiPen? I don't want to get shot with one if I don't need it."

"Good point." Every gamer in the place probably had an EpiPen. I sank even lower. "This waiting is going to kill me. Juniper needs us."

Merlin look a sip from a Big Gulp, then leaned on the counter. "Hey, Ralph." A skinny guy in a Thor T-shirt had entered the store. "Did you see the new comic by Zenith? It's about Pandora."

I sat bolt upright. "Hello? Did you say Pandora?" I scrambled to my feet. "You mean like in Pandora's box?"

"You're familiar with Greek mythology?" Merlin asked with a surprised smile. He held up the comic. "This is Zenith's tenth book. In my humble opinion, it's his opus."

According to legend, Pandora was the first woman on earth. She was famous because she opened a box and released evil into the world. But it was her daughter, Pyrrha, who most interested me, since she'd been the original owner of the urn.

"Can I see that?" I grabbed the comic and flipped through the pages. The drawings were very detailed, all in black and white. Everyone was wearing tunics and sandals. The main character was beautiful, with long rippling hair. I showed it to Ethan. "I wonder if Pandora looked like this."

"I doubt it," Ralph said, peering over my shoulder. His breath smelled like Fritos. "That armor she's wearing is medieval. If Pandora had worn armor, I'm guessing it would have been pre-Mycenaean in design. Zenith takes liberties with historical detail."

"You make an excellent point," Merlin said.

Historical detail? I set the comic book on the counter and looked from Merlin to Ralph. "You guys are talking like this stuff is real." Of course, Ethan and I knew the truth, but these guys hadn't seen a tornado fly out of an urn.

Merlin scratched his beard. "To quote one of the greatest twentieth-century minds, Mr. Spock, 'Once you have eliminated the impossible, whatever remains, however improbable, must be the truth.'" He took another sip of his drink.

"That's not technically correct," Ethan whispered to me. "Spock can't be a great mind because he's a fictitious character."

"But it kinda makes sense," I said. Then a cheer arose from the back room. Most of the players had gathered around Tyler's table. "And I swing for the win!" Tyler exclaimed. Everyone applauded. His young opponent burst into tears and fled the scene.

"It's over?" I handed the comic back to Merlin. "Tyler!" I called, pushing my way between players as they swarmed out of the game cave. Ethan followed, his baseball brim pulled low to hide his eyes.

The cave had no windows. The walls had been painted black and the air felt warm and humid, as if every molecule had been exhaled by the players. Tyler was still seated at a table, gathering his cards. "Greetings, dweebs. What's up?"

I sat on the table, my legs swinging with excitement. "We found Juniper!"

"Well, actually, she found us," Ethan said.

"She found us, we found her, what does it matter? The point is, we know where she is."

Tyler wrapped a rubber band around his deck. "Where is she?"

"At the Ladies of . . . something something, in Boston."

"The Sisters of Mercy Convalescent Center," Ethan said.

"Yeah, that's the place." His ability to remember details was like a superpower. I looked around to see if anyone was listening. Lots of people had already shuffled out of the store, but a few stood around Merlin, looking at the new comic book. "The nurse said Juniper had a stroke. But we think she's faking because she wants a place to hide."

"*You* think she's faking," Ethan corrected. "A stroke is a blood clot in the brain. To get that diagnosis, they'd have to take an image of the brain. You can't fake—"

"I think, you think . . . whatever. Yeesh." I squirmed. Sometimes he was way too literal. "I think she needs us. I have a feeling."

Tyler's whole body stiffened. "I don't want to see her. She got us into enough trouble already."

"I agree," Ethan said. "I vote we stay away from Boston. I've got an appointment with my allergist on Wednesday. I'm supposed to start my shots."

"Are you saying your allergies are more important than the fate of the world?" I looked around again. No one was paying any attention to us. I'm sure that debating the fate of the world was an everyday event in Merlin's Comics. "We saw the urn's power unleashed on four people. What would happen if it was unleashed on a hundred? A thousand? What if Juniper needs help hiding it?"

Tyler's eyes widened. "I'm not getting anywhere near that thing. Not ever again." He pushed his messy hair away from his face. "It . . . it was in my head."

"What do you mean it was in your head?" Ethan asked.

Tyler closed his eyes for a moment. When he opened them, his voice was super quiet, as if his own words scared him. "I could hear it. Not like an actual voice—that would be crazy. But like a presence, telling me to give up. Telling me that nothing was important."

I nodded. "I heard it too, when I was carrying it around. It told me to be its protector."

We shared a knowing look. It was weird having this bond with Tyler. The "Greek Urn Talking in My Head Club" wasn't one I wanted to belong to. Girl Scouts had been bad enough, with the stress of having to sell cookies and go to all those meetings. I didn't need *another* club!

I understood why Tyler hadn't admitted the voice. His mom was a psychologist. If she knew, she'd want to do some kind of scan or test Tyler's brain chemistry. She'd probably put him on medication. Or perform a lobotomy!

"I know you don't want to get anywhere near the urn," I told Tyler. "Neither do I. But what if Juniper wasn't able to hide or destroy it? Or what if she really did have a stroke and the urn is sitting around, unprotected? If someone else opens it . . ." I paused, then touched Tyler's arm. "We can't let what happened to you happen to other people."

Tyler's shoulders slumped. "Do *not* ask me to drive you."

"Would you please drive us?" I said, as if each word was coated in sugar.

He groaned. "The answer is no. Negatory. Never." He grabbed his deck, stood, then walked toward the exit.

"Hey," Merlin called. "We'll get your name engraved, then you can pick up the trophy next week."

"Have your people call my people," Tyler said with a smirk. "See ya next time, *losers*." He pushed open the door and walked across the parking lot. Ethan and I hurried after him. As he pulled his keys from his pocket, I raced ahead and threw myself in front of his car door. Then I cringed because I hated what I was about to do.

"Please," I begged. "Please, please, please take us to Boston. We need you. This is important."

Tyler scowled and pointed a key at me. "I'm done with Juniper and that urn. Do you hear me? I will never—"

"Tyler?"

We all turned and looked back at Merlin's Comics. A red-haired girl stood in the doorway. She wore a pair of shorts and Greek gladiator sandals that wound up to her knees. Her hair was styled in dozens of braids that swayed as she strode toward us.

Then I saw something I thought I'd never see. And it practically blew my mind.

The girl kissed Tyler's cheek.

5
ETHAN

FACT: *Mental chronometry is the study of response time. For example, how long does it take someone to react to a flashing Don't Walk sign, a blaring fire alarm, or the first tremors of an earthquake? It has been proven that people with higher IQs tend to score higher on reaction-time tests. But in this particular case it wasn't true. Tyler was just standing there, staring. A girl had just kissed him. Well, she'd kissed his cheek. But that counts.*

"What. Just. Happened?" Jax whispered to me.

I admit I had no explanation. Why someone would kiss my brother was beyond me. And she was pretty. Really pretty. Her red hair sparkled as if she'd sprinkled it with glitter.

Jax and I watched, dumbfounded, as the girl stepped back and smiled at Tyler. His cheeks turned red. Did Tyler have a girlfriend we didn't know about? If so, then why was he staring into space and not saying anything? Finally, the silence was broken. "I offer my congratulations to the champion," she said in a weird accent.

Oh, it was a congratulatory kiss. I guess that made sense.

She had super-long brown legs and her T-shirt was plain and white. A tan leather bag was slung over her shoulder. "Your strategy was both clever and ruthless," she said, still smiling at Tyler. "A winning combination."

"Uh-huh," he mumbled, a goofy look spreading across his face.

"I would like to learn from a great master. Might we sit together and talk?"

"Okay." His face got even redder. It wasn't like my brother to speak in one-word sentences. Or to stand like a statue. "Now?"

Jax put her hands on her hips. "Tyler, we've got something important to do."

"Is talking to me not important?" the girl asked as she batted her long eyelashes.

Tyler suddenly snapped out of it. He opened the front passenger door and started moving stuff around. "My car's usually not this messy," he lied as he tossed fast-food wrappers and comic books into the backseat.

"Tyler?" Jax said. "Hello? Great-Aunt Juniper. Remember?"

"We can go to Boston later," he grumbled.

"No, we can't. We have to go now."

"I beg your pardon," the girl said. "Why are you embarking on a journey to Boston?"

"They want me to drive them to Boston because we've got this great-aunt who's sick, but we're not sure because—" He stopped talking, thanks to a sharp whack on his shoulder from Jax. "Hey! Jeez, Jax, stop being such a brat!"

"Tyler, can we talk to you in private?" she said, shooting a nasty look at him.

The three of us walked back to Merlin's entrance, leaving the girl at the car. "Get her phone number and call her when we get back," she said, keeping her voice hushed. "The urn is more important than hanging out with her right now."

Tyler didn't look convinced. He glanced over his shoulder and waved at the girl. She waved back. "Look," he told us. "You've forgotten one important thing. You're going to need permission from the parental units if you want to go to Boston. That's a long drive. How are you going to convince them?"

Jax narrowed her eyes. "Well . . ." The answer didn't really matter. Jax had her mind set and that meant it would happen. One thing my cousin did brilliantly was get her own way. "I'm thinking. . . ." She looked around. The brick wall was covered with flyers advertising all sorts of things, from computers for sale, to upcoming concerts, to a comic-book festival in Boston. "What about that?" she said. Then she tore the flyer from its duct-taped corners and read it aloud. "International Comic Book Festival, Boston, Massachusetts."

"It's this weekend," I said, reading over Jax's shoulder. This festival would be a believable excuse. I shouldn't have been amazed. Like I said, Jax always figured out a way.

Tyler sighed. Then he waved at the girl again. The girl pointed to a store across the street. "Shall we go and eat gelato?" she called.

"Yeah, okay," he called back.

Jax grabbed Tyler's shirt hem, holding it tight so he couldn't walk away. "Look, we'll make you a deal. We'll come and get gelato with you and then you'll drive us to Boston tomorrow."

"And *why* would I want you two losers to get gelato with me and my fangirl?"

I had no answer to that question. But I could tell Jax was working out a plan in her head because her eyes were darting back and forth. "You need us, Tyler. You don't want to blow it, do you? She's clearly into you and you want to impress her, right?" He nodded. "If you tell her how great you are, she'll think you're bragging. But we can tell her all about your awards and stuff. Then she'll be so impressed, she'll practically beg you for a real date."

"Impressive logic," he said. "Fine. Help me make an irresistible impression. Then we'll talk to the parents about Boston. But I want to make one thing perfectly clear—I'm not getting anywhere near that urn. You got that?"

Jax hugged him. "Thanks, Tyler." Then he strode across the lot.

"Why do we have to get gelato with them?" I whispered to Jax. "I don't want to talk about Tyler's awards."

"Me neither," Jax whispered back. "But did you see how stupid he got around her? It's like she turned his brain to Jell-O. He might tell her something about the urn. We have to supervise."

I blew my nose again. The idea of *supervising* my older brother was as unappealing as the wad of used tissues in my pocket.

As I followed Jax across the parking lot, something started to bug me. Not the fact that my brother had attracted the attention of a really pretty girl. Not the fact that Jax was going to drag us all on another crazy adventure. It was something else. I was sure I'd never met the girl before but . . .

The way she spoke was eerily *familiar*.

6
JAX

Chatham's Creamery had been in business for a long time, and it looked like it. Mom told me that the lime-green walls and orange chairs were popular way back in the 1970s. The guy behind the counter was Gus, the owner. He had one of the biggest guts I'd ever seen, probably because the only exercise he got was scooping the gelato, which didn't look difficult because it was pretty soft stuff. My favorite flavor? Lemon ice. Ethan always got vanilla bean.

One of the differences between me and my cousins is that they always had money in their pockets, while I never did. So Ethan often got stuck paying for my share of the bill. He never complained. He was very generous. But it made me feel bad. I'm not a mooch. I just don't have access to two parents who supply twenty-dollar bills. It's like they have a cash machine in their house.

Ethan paid for my gelato, and Tyler paid for the girl's, which I guess made it an official "date." Okay, I have to admit that if you looked past the grungy clothes and the armpit stains, the messy hair and the stubble, Tyler wasn't bad-looking. And I guess if you're a gamer girl, you'd be attracted to the gaming champion.

When we got to the table, Tyler pulled out a chair for the girl. The only time he'd done that for me was as a prank so I'd fall on my butt. Guess the "Impress the Girl" show was beginning. She sat. Then we sat. Everyone took a bite of gelato. Tyler used a napkin, instead of his sleeve, to wipe chocolate from his mouth. A napkin!

The hidden truth was this—even though Tyler didn't normally have good manners, he *was* impressive. Last month, he'd proven himself to be a true hero, in every sense of the word. He'd risked his life to save me, Ethan, and Great-Aunt Juniper. He had no idea what would happen when we opened that urn, but he'd taken the risk anyway. In that moment, he'd revealed his true self. He cared about his little brother and cousin.

"How is your gelato?" Tyler asked, using his napkin again.

"Most delicious," the girl replied. "As good as anything on Mount Olympus."

Oh perfect. She was a Greek god geek, just like Tyler.

She dipped her spoon into her scoop of caramel swirl and took another bite. Then she rested her chin in her hand and smiled dreamily at him. "How did you become the champion of the game Magic: The Gathering?"

Tyler immediately launched into an explanation of the strategy he'd used to win the tournament, which was totally boring but the girl looked like she was hanging on every word. Then, before Ethan or I got the chance to talk, Tyler started listing all his other accomplishments and trophies. I must admit that even I was impressed, and I'd seen the trophies a zillion times. But this wasn't a job interview—this was a date and the conversation needed to be two-sided. I don't really know why my cousin Ethan has to go to a counselor and learn

49

social skills, because I think Tyler needs it a million times more.

I kicked Tyler under the table so he would stop talking about himself. He glared at me. I nodded my head at the girl. He shrugged. So I turned toward her and changed the subject. "How do you get your hair so sparkly?" I asked.

"I do not understand this question," she said.

"What kind of product do you use?" I touched my own hair. "To get all those sparkles? Is it a leave-in conditioner? Do you use a hot iron to keep it that straight?"

"I do not use anything."

"Oh, right. It's just *natural*." What. A. Liar. Guess she was putting on an act for Tyler. Wouldn't they both be disappointed after a few dates when they started revealing their true selves? He'd be wiping barbecue sauce off his chin with his sleeve and she'd be totally *not* sparkling. I drummed my fingers on the table. Let's get this over with so we can do the important stuff, like start packing for Boston. "So, where are you from? I don't recognize your accent."

Ethan stopped eating and looked up.

The girl fiddled with her spoon. "I am from Greece."

50

Tyler nearly choked on a piece of waffle cone. "Seriously? Greece? Did you know that my friends and I are designing a game that takes place in Greece? Well, on Mount Olympus. In the Realm of the Gods."

As Tyler told the girl all about it, I leaned close to Ethan. "Jeez," I whispered. "She's a gamer girl, she's from Greece, *and* she's not a troll. He hit the jackpot today."

"She seems nice," he whispered back.

Tyler was still talking. "Things have been slow with the game since I got back from the hospital. We need to iron out some problems we're having with—"

"Why were you in a hospital?" the girl interrupted.

"I was sick. Super sick." He took a bite of his waffle cone. "They said it was a virus. But don't worry. I'm not contagious."

She leaned her elbows on the table and stared into his eyes. "The virus . . . it made you sad. Very sad."

He nodded, his face going pale. "How did you know?"

Ethan and I held our spoons in midair, waiting

for her answer. She reached across the table and touched his arm. "I can sense this sadness. You still carry it within you."

"No, I don't," he said, squaring his shoulders. "It's gone. I'm fine."

The date had taken a serious turn, and Tyler was looking uncomfortable. I was going to try to lighten things by asking the girl about her cool shoes, but she spoke first. "You said that you were going on a journey to Boston. When do you depart?"

"Tomorrow," Tyler said.

"We're going to this thingy." I pulled the flyer from my pocket. "The International Comic Book Festival."

"Perhaps I could journey with you," the girl said.

"That would be great!" Tyler practically fell off his chair. "There's so much to see. We could check out the Puzzle Master. She helped me last year when I was having trouble with a component in Cyclopsville. She's awesome. And we could—"

"Tyler," I interrupted. "I don't think that's a good idea. What about . . . the other thing we have to do?"

The girl cocked her head. "Will you be going to the festival before or after you visit your great-aunt?"

I frowned. There was no one to blame but myself. I'd let that little bit of information slip when we were standing in the parking lot.

"You said she was sick. Did she contract the same . . . *virus*?" She was still touching his arm.

"She's had a stroke," Tyler told her. "She's at a hospital."

"Sisters of Mercy Convalescent Center," Ethan corrected. I cringed. Then he cringed, realizing that maybe he shouldn't have revealed that.

"It's a *family* thing," I said, trying to maintain some secrecy. Yeesh, what was with these guys? A pretty girl and they just start blabbing.

"I am very sorry to hear that your great-aunt is at the Sisters of Mercy Convalescent Center in Boston." She leaned forward, her eyes widening. "Will she die?"

"Maybe," Tyler said. "We don't know if she actually had a stroke. Jax thinks she's pretending."

The girl narrowed her eyes. "Pretending?"

"It's possible," I said. "People pretend things. They lie about things." I looked at her hair. *That's*

53

right, I'm looking at the sparkles that just naturally grow on your head.

Ethan cleared his throat. "Look, I just want to point out, once again, that the hospital would not have sent Juniper to Sisters of Mercy unless she'd had a stroke. They would have taken a CAT scan. You can't fake a CAT scan."

Were we going to argue about this again? I turned to Ethan and was about to explain . . . but then I realized that the girl was walking toward the exit.

"Hey," Tyler called. "Where are you going? Do you want to meet at the festival?"

"Sorry to leave but I need to do something," she said without turning around. Then she was out the door.

I crunched my paper bowl and threw it into the recycling. Tyler looked deflated, his shoulders slumped. "Maybe she had an appointment or something." I wanted to make him feel better. But she sure looked like she was in a hurry to get away from us.

"Did her voice sound familiar to you guys?" Ethan asked.

"Not really." I didn't know anyone from Greece, so I wasn't familiar with the accent. "You mean like someone from television or the movies?"

"Maybe," he said. "It's really bugging me."

Tyler looked out the shop window. The girl had already crossed the street and was disappearing around the corner of the pharmacy. Even though he was trying to hide it, he looked super disappointed.

"Just call her," I said.

"I didn't get her number."

"That's no big deal." I elbowed Ethan. "We can find her number, right? Ethan can find anything on his phone. What's her name?"

Tyler scratched his stubbly chin. We looked at each other.

Oops. No one had bothered to ask her name.

7
ETHAN

FACT: *Everyone in my family loves costumes, except me.*

I've hated costumes since the second grade, when Mom dressed me as a bumblebee and dropped me off at school. It was Halloween day but she hadn't read the latest email explaining that costumes were no longer a school tradition, thanks to a kid who'd hit another kid over the head with a toy sword. After Mom dropped me off, I learned a major life lesson— there is no way to blend in, no way to hide, not even in the corner, if you wear fluorescent yellow.

That's why I almost choked on a string bean when

Dad asked, "What costume are you going to wear to the comic-book convention, Ethan?" We were sitting at the kitchen table, eating dinner.

"Uh . . . I'm not going to wear a costume."

"You have to wear one." He leaned over and patted my knee. "You'll blend in better."

"No, I won't. I'll look stupid," I said.

"At a comic-book convention, the people not wearing costumes are the ones who look stupid," Dad said. "Am I right?"

"Like freaks," Tyler said, then stuffed an egg roll into his mouth. We were eating Chinese takeout— something we always did when Mom was away on business. My parents owned Rainbow Product Testing, and their main clients were toy manufacturers. Mom was in Chicago at an educational-toy fair and would be gone until next week.

"You're saying that if I go to the convention in a pair of jeans and a shirt, and I'm surrounded by guys dressed like My Little Pony, I'm the one who'll feel like a weirdo?"

"Uh-huh." Tyler's mouth was full.

"I don't think so." I scooped more fried rice onto my plate.

"At least wear a cape," Dad said.

"Yeah." Tyler snorted. "You can go as Factoid Boy."

It had been way too easy to lie to Dad. He'd taken one look at the flyer and said, "Sounds like fun. When are you leaving?" He'd gone to dozens of comic-book conventions over the years. His Batman collection was even larger than Tyler's. I hated lying to him. So I promised myself that after we saw Great-Aunt Juniper, we would go to the convention, even if only for five minutes, just to make things right.

The television was on in the study. I could see it through the open door. I'd turned the volume down but I kept looking around my dad's shoulder to read the news feed at the bottom of the screen. My favorite stories were the ones about weather—freak storms, hurricane warnings, and anything to do with global warming. But the current story had to do with a tax increase.

Mom had only been gone a day but I missed her. Not just because she liked to watch the news with me, but because she'd tell Tyler to forget about going to Boston. He needed more time to recover from the "mysterious virus." He needed rest. If Mom were here, she would be our excuse to not go.

As if reading my mind, Dad set his fork aside and looked at Tyler. "Your mom's still worried about your health." He rested his elbows on the table. "How are you feeling? Are you sure you're up to taking this trip?"

Tyler glanced quickly at me. Then he grabbed another egg roll. "Yeah, no problem." He fake smiled at Dad. There was no mention of voices or darkness. I never knew my brother was such a good actor. "I'm totally back to normal."

"Great." Dad patted Tyler's shoulder.

He didn't ask if we needed a hotel. Dad didn't seem to care about things like that. Don't get me wrong. He was a good dad, but the only time he worried about details was in his lab.

But I was already wondering where we'd stay, and what time we'd leave.

Dad grabbed his plate and headed for the sink. "I wish I could go with you but I've got a report that can't be delayed." Then he went upstairs to his office.

"Guess we're going," I said with a sigh.

Tyler looked equally unhappy about the situation. He grumbled something about Jax and her stupid secret-box birthday present, then crammed another egg roll into his mouth.

A special report appeared on the television screen. While Tyler chewed, I read the streaming headline.

STRANGE BANK ROBBERY IN NEW YORK CITY. EMPLOYEES ACTED LIKE ZOMBIES.

Huh?

I walked into the study and sat in the leather chair. Then I turned up the volume. "We don't have all the facts, but we do know that the robbery took place approximately one hour ago, at the Excelsior bank in Manhattan." The news reporter stood across the street from the bank. Ambulances were lined up behind her. A police officer was shouting at people to stay behind the yellow tape. "According to one of the paramedics, the bank's interior looks like it was hit by a windstorm. Papers are scattered everywhere. Windows are shattered as if a tornado had been unleashed."

Tornado?

"Tyler!" I hollered. "Tyler, get in here! Hurry!"

Tyler rushed in, a dumpling speared on the end of his fork. "What?" He stared at the screen.

The news reporter continued. "The security cameras recorded a man entering the bank just a few minutes before closing time. He was holding a leather bag. When he opened the bag, the cameras shattered, indicating the possible presence of a bomb, or some sort of terrorist weapon; we aren't certain at this point. What we do know is that whatever he had in that bag, it unleashed a powerful force that smashed glass and toppled furniture, but did not kill anyone."

Tyler dropped his fork. His jaw went slack.

"Police have released this photograph of the suspect and are issuing a warning that he should not be approached. He could have another weapon." A grainy photograph filled the screen. The man was dressed in a black shirt and black pants. He was tall and skinny and wore a fedora. But his face was hidden behind the collar of his shirt.

"According to the same paramedic, the bank staff and three customers who were inside during the robbery are all suffering from unusual physical symptoms. He described them as zombies."

Tyler sank onto the couch, his face going white.

My hand, still holding the remote, began to tremble. Then my phone rang.

"Ethan?" Jax said on the other end of the line, her voice breathless. "Did you see the news?"

"Yes," I replied.

"Do you know what this means?" She didn't wait for my response. But I knew. And Tyler knew. That's why we were both staring at the TV screen, our mouths hanging open.

"That bank robber has Great-Aunt Juniper's urn."

8
JAX

A bank robber was using Juniper's urn for evil. Who was he? And how had he gotten the urn? Is that why Juniper was at Sisters of Mercy, pretending to have had a stroke? I knew it! I knew she was hiding. Tomorrow we'd go to Boston and get some answers. I hated waiting. It made me feel jittery, like when I drank coffee, which I didn't do very often. I had enough energy without adding caffeine.

I turned on my computer. Ever since we'd gotten back from Washington, DC, I'd started keeping a journal. It felt too dangerous to write on paper, especially since my mom liked to go on cleaning sprees and attack every inch of my room. So I created a document with a password—Pandorasbox.

And I wrote and wrote and wrote. I wanted to keep track of the events. I tried to remember every word Great-Aunt Juniper had said about the urns— where they'd come from, how she'd found them. If a stranger hacked into this file, he'd think I was writing a story for English class. No one could possibly think it had actually happened!

As I wrote in my journal, I'd check my inbox, hoping to see an email from Juniper. There were so many questions I wanted to ask her, so many gaps in the story. But most of all, I wanted to know that she was safe.

But nothing came. Day after day had passed with no contact from her.

And then that single email had arrived.

FROM: Juniper
TO: Jacqueline Malone
SUBJECT: How Are You?

I'd opened it, but it was empty. Nothing. Had she started to contact me, then changed her mind?

But that night, after convincing Mom to let me go to Boston, and after watching the terrible news story about the bank robber, I got an email I never expected.

FROM: Isaac Romero

TO: Jacqueline Malone

SUBJECT: I'm Your Father

When I first read it, my stomach went into a knot. Was this some sort of trick? Normally I wouldn't open an email from someone I didn't know, and technically, I didn't *know* him. I'd spent most of my life not even hearing his name. Mom always told me he was someone she'd dated briefly, nothing more. She'd raised me on her own. Even though I'd asked about him lots and lots of times, she'd never told me the truth.

But then I met Great-Aunt Juniper, and it turned out she knew the truth about my father— that he was a professional thief. Mom had tried to protect me from the truth. Or maybe she was trying to protect herself from embarrassment. I'm not sure.

It turned out he'd been arrested. And he chose not to contact her, or tell her where he was, which is pretty cruddy. And so, I grew up not knowing him.

But now I knew the truth. And thanks to the internet, he'd found my address.

So I opened it.

Dear Jacqueline,

It must seem strange to hear from me after all of these years. How are you?

Your father, Isaac Romero

When I read that, I felt faint. I had to make sure this wasn't some kind of identity-stealing trick, so I wrote back.

FROM: Jacqueline Malone

TO: Isaac Romero

SUBJECT: Hello

Dear Mr. Romero,

I am fine but how do I know that you are who you say you are?

Sincerely, Jax

The reply took only a minute.

FROM: Isaac Romero

TO: Jacqueline Malone

SUBJECT: Re: Hello

Dear Jacqueline, I met your mother while I was working for your great-aunt Juniper. And I made you a special box, which Juniper mailed to you for your birthday. I hope that information proves to you that I am your father. I am currently incarcerated at Brookville Federal Prison Camp in Rhode Island. I am not allowed to make phone calls.

It was him! My father was contacting me!

I didn't call Ethan and tell him what was going on. Perhaps that was a mistake but the truth was, I was ashamed. Ethan's father was a great guy who spent time with his kids, did all the things fathers are supposed to do. And my dad was in jail. I wanted to talk to him without anyone knowing. This felt very private.

So I googled the prison and here's what I learned. Brookville Federal Prison Camp was called a camp because it was a minimum-security prison. If you're not a violent threat to society, you might go to one of those places. I read an article by a man who'd been in Brookville. Most of the Brookville inmates had committed "white collar" crimes—which meant they were greedy thieves but they weren't violent. Prison camps are sometimes called Club Fed because they have things like tennis courts, running tracks, weight rooms, and libraries. The article was all about how the biggest problem inside was finding ways to fill the endless hours. Many inmates took classes. Some chose to work jobs they would have never worked on the outside, like in the kitchen, or doing clerical work or gardening. Reading was a favorite activity. Friends and family could send books to the inmates, but only paperbacks. I wondered if my dad liked to read travel guides. Did we have that in common?

There were so many things I wanted to tell him. Luckily, Mom was already asleep. So I started writing.

FROM: Jacqueline Malone
TO: Isaac Romero
SUBJECT: Re: Hello
Dear Mr. Romero,
It is nice to hear from you. I never
knew your name or anything about you.
Great-Aunt Juniper gave me the box
that you made. It was really nice. We
figured out how to open it. Thank you
for making it. I am twelve years old

now, but you probably know that. Why
are you in prison? And when do you get
out?

The response came quickly.

FROM: Isaac Romero
TO: Jacqueline Malone
SUBJECT: Juniper
Dear Jacqueline,
You are very welcome for the box. I
am glad that your great-aunt sent it
to you. She is a very nice person. I
enjoyed working for her. I would like
to talk to her. Where is she?

Where is she? I sat back in my desk chair. Should
I answer that question? Great-Aunt Juniper and
the urn were the biggest secrets of my life. Just
because Isaac Romero and I shared DNA didn't
mean I could trust him.

I could never tell Mom that my father was email-
ing me. She was still mad at him and at Juniper. And
she was mad at me because, a few weeks before my
birthday, I'd gotten caught shoplifting a candy bar.
I'd just wanted to see if I could get away with it and

I was going to put it back on the shelf, but I wasn't quick enough. Mom kept lecturing me about fighting my urges to steal. I told her I didn't have any urges to steal, which was the truth.

I would never follow in my father's footsteps. I wish she'd get that out of her head.

But there were certain things I couldn't get out of my head. Like . . . did I look like him? Did I act, talk, or walk like him? And why, after so many years, was he finally writing to me?

I did know that Great-Aunt Juniper trusted him. She'd told us as much. But I needed to check with her first. She was in hiding, after all.

FROM: Jacqueline Malone
TO: Isaac Romero
SUBJECT: Re: Juniper
Dear Mr. Romero,
I can't tell you where she is but I am going to see her tomorrow. I will give her your email address. I have to go to sleep because we are leaving early. Bye for now. Jax.

9
ETHAN

FACT: *Zombies are scientifically impossible.*

In theory, zombies are animated corpses, which means that the person dies and then some magical force reanimates the body and makes it walk around. But even though the body is technically dead, it still wants to eat. That doesn't make sense. Tyler used to talk about the zombie apocalypse. It's supposed to be caused by a plague that spreads all over the globe and turns us all into a mass of mindless undead. But we'd still be hungry.

It annoyed me when the reporter used the term "zombies" to describe those people inside Excelsior

Bank. No one had died during the robbery, so no one had been reanimated. Therefore, they couldn't be zombies. I wish news people would check their facts before scaring viewers.

It was Saturday, the morning after the robbery. I'd barely slept because I'd been watching my phone all night for updates. If the robber had Juniper's urn, this could be the beginning of a crime spree the likes of which had never been seen. Or *felt*. As my English teacher would say—a dark foreshadowing of things to come.

Why did Jax always drag me into these things?

Before we picked her up, Tyler stopped at Starbucks and got a triple-shot latte. I'm not a coffee drinker, and the last thing Jax needed was caffeine, so I bought two Italian sodas, raspberry flavored. Tyler didn't say much. He yawned between sips. Maybe he hadn't slept either. Maybe he'd been awake all night, reliving that moment in the Jefferson Memorial. When he started talking, it was all about the girl.

"Why didn't I ask her name? Maybe she'll show up at the next Magic tournament. Oh, I bet the guys at Merlin's would know who she is. Let's go ask."

"We don't have time," I said. We were already fifteen minutes late. Jax would be waiting.

My mom, the psychologist, would probably think it was a good sign that Tyler was showing interest in a girl. He'd never had a girlfriend. Neither had I, unless you counted the two days in sixth grade when Anna Marie Bacon pretended to be my girlfriend to make this guy named Max jealous. We were all in the same social-skills workshop. She kept hugging me and clinging to my arm. I told Anna Marie that she was breaking the personal-space rule, but she didn't care. She made me so nervous, I stayed home the rest of the week with a fake stomachache. When I came back to school on Monday, she told me she didn't want to be tied down to one guy and that she was breaking up with me. It was one of the happiest days of my life.

I think the main reason Mom agreed to let Tyler drive us on this latest quest, despite his recent illness, was because she wanted Tyler to get out of the house more often. She told him this all the time. "Why don't you go do something?" was one of her favorite things to say.

Ten minutes after leaving the Starbucks parking lot, Tyler pulled into Jax's driveway. We waited while she hugged her mom good-bye. Then she tossed her purple jacket and backpack onto the car floor. "You guys are totally late," she grumbled as she climbed in next to me. "I've been waiting for hours."

"Twenty-five minutes," I corrected, double-checking my phone. "Okay, twenty-six."

Tyler rolled down the driver's window and had a long discussion with Aunt Lindsay, assuring her that he would drive carefully, that he wouldn't let us out of his sight, and that he'd call her with updates. Aunt Lindsay handed Tyler a box of day-old pastries from the diner. He immediately shoved an almond Danish into his mouth. Then Aunt Lindsay tapped on the back window. Jax rolled it down. "Don't worry," my aunt said to me. "Jax won't leave your side." She smiled in a motherly way. "Have fun!" she hollered as we backed out of the driveway.

"Leave my side?" I asked as I handed Jax an Italian soda.

"She was totally suspicious," Jax explained. "Why would I want to go to a comic-book thingy? Mom knows I never read comic books. So I told her that you'd begged me to go because you were freaking out about the huge crowd. She knows how you get."

"Oh." I guess that was a good excuse. Everyone in the family knew I hated crowds.

"Thanks for the soda." She took a long sip. "You

guys didn't tell your parents anything about Juniper, right?"

"Not a word," I said.

"Nada from me," Tyler said.

Jax swirled her straw. The raspberry syrup turned the whipped cream pink. "I don't like all this lying."

I didn't like it either. I was the world's worst liar. It was hard enough to make eye contact during a regular conversation. When I lied, my mouth started to fill with spit so I had to swallow really fast. I think that looks very suspicious.

"So, what's the news on the robbery?" Jax asked.

I'd been checking my phone all morning for updates. "Excelsior Bank is under quarantine," I said. "The shops around it are also closed. At first they were worried about radioactivity, but now the police suspect a biological weapon. But they can't explain the wind. The security cameras recorded the storm before they were shattered. The Center for Disease Control is sending in investigators."

"They'll never figure it out," Tyler said. "How could they? They'd have to think outside the box."

Jax set her soda into the cup holder. "Even if they caught the thief and opened the urn themselves, they'd never guess it was made by Zeus."

"Maybe it would be better if the police had the urn. Then at least it wouldn't be in a criminal's hands," I said. Once again, I was trying to be the voice of reason. "They would treat it as a terrorist weapon. They'd lock it up so it couldn't hurt other people."

"Maybe," Jax said. "But if the government knew about it, they could use it for political reasons. And what if a terrorist got his hands on it?"

"War," Tyler said. He gripped the steering wheel. He was the only one among us who knew how it felt to be completely hopeless. "Someone has to destroy it," he said, his voice cold.

He was right. But did that someone have to be one of us?

We were on the freeway, with a three-and-one-half-hour drive ahead of us. I kept checking to see if anyone was following. The Camels were in prison, in England, so they couldn't bother us anymore. But they could send someone else. I was too nervous to read the book I'd brought—the latest edition of *Guinness World Records*.

"How did the bank robber get the urn from Juniper? That's what I want to know." Jax grabbed a powdered-sugar doughnut from the box. "We've got to talk to her. Can't you go faster?"

I cringed. Tyler could drive a virtual vehicle through any kind of obstacle course, but in the real world, it had taken him three tries to pass his driving test. "CNN said that motor vehicle crashes are the leading cause of death among teenagers," I pointed out. "Besides, if he gets a ticket, he'll lose his driving privileges. Mom and Dad are still mad about that broken window." During our trip to Washington, DC, Mr. and Mrs. Camel stole the secret box from Tyler's car by breaking the window.

Jax groaned. "When is someone going to invent a faster way to travel?"

"The fastest way to travel on land is on a rocket sled," I said, taking full advantage of this factoid opportunity. "It's pretty cool because it slides along a set of rails, like a train, but it's propelled by rockets. It holds the land-based speed record at Mach eight point five."

Jax slumped against the seat. "Whatever. Just make sure we don't take a wrong turn, okay?"

"Okay." As usual, I was in charge of the mapping. Tyler's car was too old to have an onboard navigation system. That was fine by me because I don't like that lady's voice. Even though I know it's prerecorded, it still sounds like she gets mad if you miss a turn. And if she gives you the wrong directions, you can't correct her. "Two hundred and thirty miles to go," I said. Jax groaned.

Then, to my surprise, she pulled a book from her backpack. She wasn't a big reader. The only books she carried around were travel guides she'd collected from garage sales. She liked to fantasize about all the places she'd visit when she was rich and famous. But this book's title was *A Collection of Greek Myths*. "I've been reading as much as I can about Pandora and her family." She opened the book to an illustration of a woman in a toga, holding a box. "Here she is," she said. It looked more realistic than the comic-book picture we saw back at Merlin's. She held it up so Tyler could see it in the rearview mirror. Then she turned the page to a woman with snakes growing out of her head.

"Medusa," Tyler said, his gaze darting between the road and the mirror. "She turns people to stone." He knew everything about Greek myths. Jax turned another page. "That's Pan. He's a Satyr. Half goat, half human. He was the demi-god of the woodlands."

Jax leaned over the front seat. "If Pandora and her family really lived, does that mean that all these stories are true? Does that mean that Pan is real? And Cyclopses too?"

"*Were* real," I corrected.

"What do you think, Tyler? Do you think they had green blood, just like in your game?"

Tyler reached for another pastry. "If Cyclopses are real, little cousin, then the line between fantasy and reality will need to be redrawn."

"*Were* real," I said again. Why couldn't they get that straight?

"Verb tense is the least of our worries," Tyler said. Then he shoved half a croissant into his mouth.

I mumbled to myself that verb tense was important. It was difficult for me to accept that what I had once considered to be fiction might now be fact. I frowned, then checked my phone. "Two hundred and twenty more miles."

Jax groaned and sank low on the seat. "Where's a rocket sled when you need one?"

10
JAX

Finally! After a million hours in the car, we reached the Sisters of Mercy Convalescent Center.

Ethan almost drove me crazy. Don't get me wrong, I really love him. He is my best friend. But four hours of trivia made my brain feel like it had been pricked with needles. Tyler finally snapped. "If you don't shut it, I'm going to stuff a day-old doughnut in your mouth." Ethan grumbled something about how no one ever appreciated him, then he plugged earbuds into his phone and listened to the news. It wasn't true. I appreciated him. Except for all that sneezing and nose blowing.

Tyler took forever to find a parking spot. I think he was stalling. I didn't blame him for not wanting to see Juniper again. For almost a month, he'd been a different person, and the urn had been to blame. But it had been my birthday present; so, in a way, I was also to blame. Sometimes I was angry at our great-aunt for sending me that urn. And other times I was grateful, because now I had proof that magic truly existed. I'd always suspected as much.

Without the urn, I might have never learned the truth about my dad.

Sisters of Mercy was a small brick building. The walkway was lined with blue pansies and the lawn was bright green and perfectly mowed. A bronze statue of a nun stood in the center of the yard, her palms pressed together in prayer. A few patients sat in the shade of a big oak tree. They'd fallen asleep in their wheelchairs.

"I can't find a place to stay," Ethan said as Tyler set the parking brake. "Every hotel and motel is booked. The only vacancies are penthouse suites or bridal suites and they're super expensive."

Thanks to the comic-book festival, a rock concert, and a car show, Boston was packed. "Don't worry. I told Mom we had a room at the Best Eastern hotel," I said.

"Uh, they are called Best *Western* hotels," Tyler said.

"Whatever. She seemed fine with it. And I had to say something." Does lying to your mom not count if you're trying to save humanity?

"This is a disaster. What are we going to do?" Ethan asked, his voice cracking. He always made such a big deal out of things. "Where are we going to sleep?"

"We'll be okay," I said calmly. If we had to sleep in the car, what was the big deal? We could do it for one night. We could use a restaurant bathroom. We'd figure it out when the time came. But I didn't say those things to Ethan because he hated not having a plan. He worried about everything. I was worried about our great-aunt and the stolen urn, not where I'd brush my teeth.

"What do you think that girl's doing?" Tyler asked.

"Who cares?" I said. "Yeesh. A guy robbed a bank last night and turned the tellers into zombies. Let's think about important things."

"Not technically zombies," Ethan said.

When we got out of the car, both Ethan and I checked to make sure no one had followed us. Even though it was hot out, I put on my purple coat. It was my favorite thing to wear. It kinda felt like my adventuring uniform. Ethan tucked his phone into his back pocket. Tyler grabbed the last pastry, locked the car, then stuck his keys into his pocket. Then they followed me up the walkway.

The front door was super thick and heavy. I had to punch the handicapped button to get it to swing open. Ethan pulled his baseball cap low, hiding beneath its brim—something he always did when we were about to talk to strangers.

"Why do these places always smell so bad?" Tyler asked as we stepped inside. That was a funny comment coming from Tyler, whose bedroom smelled like a skunk's butt. Even though I'd never smelled a skunk's butt, I imagined it was pretty disgusting. I usually stayed as far away from Tyler's room as possible.

The Sisters of Mercy hallway was lined on both sides with old people in wheelchairs. Some were asleep, others were tapping their feet to music that streamed out of an open door. The sign on the door read, *Sing-along with Betty*. I peeked inside.

The room was super crowded. Warbly voices sang a Frank Sinatra song called "That Old Black Magic." I recognized it because my mom is a big Frank Sinatra fan. I assumed Betty was the woman at the piano, leading the sing-along.

"Everyone in here looks like they're about to croak," Tyler said. He hadn't even bothered to whisper.

"That's mean," I told him. "One day you're gonna be old."

"I don't think so." A bunch of pastry crumbs had gotten caught in his stubble. "I'm going to grow clones and transplant my brain as soon as my body starts to wear out." He was serious.

"Do you see Juniper?" Ethan asked, peering over my shoulder.

"No." I scanned again, just to make sure there were no long white braids or red bandanas in the crowd. "She's not in here. Let's ask someone." The reception desk was across the way. A sign read, *Visitor Check-In*.

Even though Tyler was the oldest, I'm the one who marched up to the counter. I wanted to do the talking because Ethan was a terrible liar and because Tyler was . . . well, Tyler.

"Hello," I said. "We're here to see someone." The lady behind the counter was dressed in a plain white blouse and black skirt. Her name tag read, *Sister Beatrice*.

"Hello." Before she said another word, her phone rang. "Excuse me for a moment."

I tapped my fingers on the counter as she answered the phone. She forwarded the call to someone else, then got distracted by two police officers who walked down the hall and stopped next to me.

"We just finished checking on Jane Doe, so we're headin' back to the station house now," the tall one told Sister Beatrice. "We've got a bit of paperwork to write up."

The other officer, a woman with a mole on her cheek, leaned on the counter. "If someone comes to identify her, give us a call. We don't want anyone talking to her unless there's an officer present."

I looked over at Tyler and Ethan. They'd both heard the comment. How were we supposed to talk about the urn if there was a police officer in Juniper's room?

"Why?" Sister Beatrice asked. "Is she in trouble?"

The female officer answered. "It appears that

she'd been tampering with the museum's security system just before she had her stroke. The only reason to tamper with a security system is to steal something. The museum might press charges against her. We want to monitor all her conversations, for evidence."

The other officer handed a card to Sister Beatrice. "Call us immediately if anyone comes in to see her." Then he frowned. "What's her prognosis? Is she gonna make it?"

"Her condition is not terminal," the sister replied. "But her memory is damaged. It will take time for her to recover." The officers said good-bye, then headed out the front door.

Of course she wasn't going to die. This whole thing was a big act so she could have a place to hide out.

"Sorry for the interruption," Sister Beatrice said to me. She set the card next to the phone. "Who are you visiting today?"

I glanced at the card. If I said I'd come to see Jane Doe, the police would come back. So I quickly scanned the files that were spread across the desk. One of the names caught my eye. "Herman Hoffsteder."

"Are you a family member?"

"Yes." I smiled sweetly. "My brothers and I are his family members." I pointed to Ethan and Tyler, who were still standing next to the sing-along. Then I wished I hadn't called Ethan and Tyler my brothers because we looked nothing alike. What if Sister Beatrice questioned me? Would I have to provide more details? Lying to a nun was one of the worst things I'd ever done. But lucky for me, Sister Beatrice got distracted by another phone call. She pushed a pen and a clipboard across the counter. "Sign in, please."

Out of pure habit, I started to sign, *Jax Ma* . . . but stopped. Oops. I shouldn't use my real name. What should I use? I'd often thought that if I could choose a last name, I'd choose something from one of my travel guidebooks, like London, or Paris. So I finished the signature—*Jax Madrid*. That sounded like a famous writer or designer. "What room is Uncle Herman in?" I asked, trying not to bounce on my toes. I looked at the desk again, to see if there were any notes about Jane Doe. Maybe I'd find her room number. But I found nothing.

"Herman's not in his room right now. He's over there." She pointed to a man sitting in a wheel-chair a little ways down the hall. "Herman!" she called. "You have visitors." The old man rubbed his bald head and frowned. Then Sister Beatrice's phone rang again and she started talking to somebody about medical supplies.

I walked over to Mr. Hofstedder. "Hello, Uncle Herman," I said real loud.

"Do I know you?" His eyes were so cloudy it looked like milk had been spilled on his eyeballs.

"Yes. I'm your niece, Jax." Lying to a nun *and* a nice old man—yeesh. Maybe this is the part of me that I got from my father, the criminal. I smiled and waved at Sister Beatrice but she barely noticed since she was still on the phone. I grabbed the handles of the wheelchair and started wheeling my victim down the hall. Ethan and Tyler hurried after me.

"What are you doing?" Tyler asked.

"We're taking Uncle Herman for a ride."

"I ain't your uncle." Herman grumbled. "I may be confused about what year this is, but I know I don't got any nieces or nephews. And I don't want to take no ride."

"I'm sorry," I said. "Just act like you're having fun."

"Fun?" He snorted. "I haven't had fun since they stuck me in this place."

"Do you have a plan?" Ethan asked as he

nervously looked around.

"Open every door until we find her," I said. "That's the plan."

Tyler and Ethan took one side of the hall, I took the other. I stopped at the first room and peeked in. The windowsill was decorated with porcelain figurines and doilies. The next room had lots of family photos and an orange crocheted blanket. Another nun greeted us as she pushed a cart up the hall. It was filled with medications. "Hello, Herman," she said. "Nice to see you have visitors." Her name tag read, *Sister Agnes.*

"They ain't my visitors," Herman complained. "I was minding my own business and they kidnapped me."

"That's nice," Sister Agnes said, just before turning into a room. She probably heard stuff like that all day long. How could she know Herman was telling the truth and not just confused?

A few rooms later, the hallway branched out on either side to form a T shape. I was about to tell Tyler and Ethan to take one hallway, and I'd take the other, when a door marked 19 opened. A large man stepped out. He was dressed in white pants and a white shirt. He looked like he worked there, maybe an orderly or a nurse. After closing the door, he walked down the hall and joined Sister Agnes, who was pushing her cart from another room.

"Hi, Louis. Did you just come from Jane Doe's room?"

"Yeah," Louis told her.

I'd found her! Great-Aunt Juniper was behind door number 19. It was like a game show, where you hope that the door you choose has the biggest prize.

"She's agitated," he said. "Her window was wide open. She said the gods had found her."

"Poor thing," Sister Agnes said.

The gods had found her? Wow, Juniper was really good at pretending to be confused.

"I gave her the sedative," Louis said. "She should be going to sleep soon."

Uh-oh. We needed to talk to her quick, before she fell asleep.

While they talked, I pretended to be adjusting Herman's blanket, making him more comfortable. "Leave me alone," he snapped.

"Shhh," I told him, trying my best to hear the conversation.

"Why were the police in her room?" Sister Agnes asked.

"Didn't you hear? She had her stroke at the Museum of Fine Arts. The police said she broke into the security office. But they haven't been able to figure out her motive." He took the cart and began to push it farther down the hall. Sister Agnes followed alongside. "I'm going to lunch in twenty. You want to get a fozen yogurt?"

"Oh, that sounds good," Sister Agnes said. They disappeared around the corner.

A small paper sign was taped outside room 19: *Hospital Staff Admittance Only.* "Hey," I called to Ethan and Tyler, waving them over. "This is it."

"That ain't my room," Herman Hofstedder said.

Ethan stared at the sign. "We can't go in there." I knew exactly what he'd say next—that we'd be breaking rules and that trespassing was illegal. He was right. But this was not the time to worry about rules. Louis had given a sedative to Juniper, and that meant she'd be asleep soon. We needed to get some answers now. I looked around. The hallway was empty. So I opened the door.

"I have a bad feeling about this," Ethan complained.

Mr. Hofstedder grunted. "That makes two of us."

Tyler narrowed his eyes. "What if the urn's in there?"

I'd been thinking the same thing, but how could that be possible? "The bank robber has it, remember?"

"Yeah, but what if . . . ?" Tyler's face went pale. I felt as scared as he looked, but we couldn't back down now.

"Don't worry, I don't think it's in there," I told him. "I'm not sensing anything." During our adventure in Washington, DC, I'd felt the urn's presence. Even though it had been hidden in the Camels' motel room, I'd been able to feel it calling to me. But that did not happen as I stood outside room 19. "Let's go in and talk to her."

Tyler straightened his back, as if pushing away the fear. Then he waved his arm. "After you, dweeboids."

"Watch your language, young man," Mr. Hoffsteder grumbled.

Tyler was the last inside and he closed the door behind us.

11
ETHAN

FACT: *Human cloning already exists in the form of identical twins. But that process takes place naturally.*

When Tyler says he wants to clone himself and replant his brain whenever his body wears out, he's talking about replacement cloning. It's theoretically possible that my generation could see this in our lifetime. Tyler could extend his life by generations. So could Jax and I. Which means Tyler would be calling us dweeboids for a very long time.

But Juniper couldn't have a brain transplant. So we could only hope that the damage she'd suffered from her stroke was reversible. That her brain would repair itself. Jax was wrong about her not having a stroke.

The room was sparse, with one bed, one dresser, and a television set. There were no personal items like in the other rooms. She lay on the bed, metal handlebars perched on both sides. I guess they were meant to protect her so she wouldn't fall out. It reminded me of a crib.

She wore a plain light-blue cotton nightgown. Her white hair was unbraided and fanned across the pillow. Her eyes were closed. Jax let go of Mr. Hofstedder's handlebars, then leaned over the bed. "Great-Aunt Juniper?" she said quietly.

Juniper's eyes popped open. "Jax!" She reached out a trembling, pale hand. "Thank the gods you're here." As Jax squeezed our great-aunt's hand, I wondered about Mr. Hofstedder. What if he had real visitors and they started looking for him?

"Shouldn't we put our *uncle* back in the hall?" I asked.

Herman Hofstedder snorted. "Yes. Put me in the hall. Leave me in peace."

"Don't put him in the hall," Jax whispered to us. "He might tell someone we're in here." Then she patted the old man's shoulder. "It'll be fine, Mr. Hofstedder. We'll take you back in a few minutes."

Juniper turned her head and looked at me, her eyes watery and red. "Who are you?" she asked.

"Uh . . . I'm Ethan."

"Of course." She nodded slowly. "Ethan and Tyler. Hello."

"How do you feel?" Jax asked her.

"They tell me I had a stroke." She spoke out of the right corner of her mouth. The left side didn't move.

"What?" Jax said, unclasping Juniper's hand. "You did? Really?"

I watched Juniper's face for a few moments. Then I noticed that her left arm lay limp. "Your left side is paralyzed, isn't it? That's a common symptom after a stroke. Just like my neighbor Mrs. Purcell." I'd been correct about the stroke. But being right didn't make me happy. She looked really terrible.

"Makes it hard to talk," Juniper said. Then she yawned with half her mouth. "How come I'm so tired?"

"The nurse gave you a pill to make you sleep," Jax told her. "I can't believe you really had a stroke. Do you remember what happened?"

Juniper brushed a few strands of hair from her

eye. "Certain things are *fuzzy*."

"Why were you at the Museum of Fine Arts?" Tyler asked. He sat on the windowsill. "The police think you were trying to steal something."

Her left eyelid was droopier than the right. "I can't remember that part. I try and try. The police asked me what I was doing there. But I don't know. It's so foggy."

This was serious. Along with the paralysis, she had an impaired memory. Jax looked at me, her brow furrowed with worry.

"We'd better tell her about the robbery," Tyler said.

"What about Mr. Hofstedder?" I asked. "Should we talk about this in front of him?"

We all looked at the old man. His head had fallen to the side and he was snoring. Jax nodded at me. So I started talking. It was easy for me to remember all the details, like time of day, number of people who'd been attacked, and the amount of money stolen.

"The robber used the urn," Jax said. "Do you know who he is? Do you remember how he got it?" Juniper half-yawned again. The sleeping pill was starting to kick in. "Great-Aunt Juniper? How did that man steal the urn from you?"

"He didn't steal it from me."

"What?" Tyler slid off the windowsill. "Are you saying you *gave* it to him?"

"No." She sighed. "It's a different urn."

I felt prickly all over. My heart skipped a couple of beats. Had I heard her correctly?

"Wait a minute." Tyler held up a hand. "Are you saying the bank robber has one of the *other* urns?"

"Yes." She blinked, slow and heavy. "He has the urn of Faith."

"Faith?" we all said.

Tyler looked frantically around the room. "Does that mean the urn of Hope is in this room? I told you, Jax, I don't want to see it!" My heart began to pound. I didn't want to see it either.

"It can't be that close," Jax said. "I don't feel anything."

"Well, I feel something!" Herman Hofstedder bellowed as he woke up. "I feel hungry. But I don't want no cruddy meat loaf again. It gave me terrible gas." He pounded his fists on his wheelchair. "If you don't let me outta this room, I'm gonna—"

"Okay, fine," Jax grumbled. She opened the door, looked into the hall to make sure no one was watching, then wheeled Mr. Hofstedder outside.

"Bye," I told him with a wave. "Have a nice day."

"So far it's been a real thrill ride," he grumbled.

As soon as the door closed, Jax, Tyler, and I gathered around our great-aunt's bed. "Where is it?" Jax asked. "Where is the urn of Hope?"

"I can't remember. I can't . . . oh yes." Juniper pointed a shaky finger at the window. "I gave it to someone."

"Gave it to someone?"

Her hand fell back onto the bed and her eyes closed. "Don't worry. We can trust her. She came from the Realm of the Gods."

"That's not possible," I said. But even as I said it, I knew that phrase didn't have as much weight as it used to.

My nose started to tingle.

12
JAX

Great-Aunt Juniper's brain was all mixed up.
I'd felt like that before. Once, when I was
little, I got so sick that I had a fever of 103. Mom
said I started talking about unicorns—I thought
one was standing in the middle of the living room!
I remember how confused I'd felt, until my fever
broke.

It was hard to see Juniper like this. I remembered all the photos in her apartment, of her
adventures trekking across the globe in search of
artifacts and treasures. She'd been strong and inde-
pendent. Now she was lying in a bed with metal
bars. I felt bad because I'd thought she was faking
the stroke.

"Did you say the *Realm of the Gods*?" I asked.

"Yes." Her eyelids fluttered.

"Cyclopsville takes place in the Realm of the Gods," Tyler said. Then he shrugged. "I'm just pointing that out."

Ethan stopped pinching his nose. "False alarm," he explained.

"I don't understand," I said to Juniper. I tried to keep my voice calm, so I wouldn't upset her. "Are you telling us that the urn of Hope was here with you, in this room?"

"Yes." Her voice was beginning to drift. "Don't worry. I sealed it with wax. At least, I think I did." She frowned, crease lines forming along her cheeks. "I told everyone that it contained my husband's ashes. I don't remember having a husband. Did I have a husband?"

"Search," I said. We opened all the drawers. There were some clothes—a pair of khaki pants, a red bandana, some hiking boots, a leather bag that was empty. We looked under the bed, in the closet, but found no dreaded Greek urn. Tyler exhaled with relief but I didn't. I grabbed Juniper's hand to get her attention. "Great-Aunt Juniper? I know it's hard to remember but please try. Are you sure you gave the urn of Hope to someone?"

She nodded weakly.

"That means it's not here," Tyler said. "Fine by me!"

Panic began to swirl in my stomach, like a cyclone. "But . . . why?"

"She said she'd take it home." Juniper closed her eyes. "I'm getting so sleepy."

"Please don't fall asleep," I begged, shaking her arm. "You gave it to a girl? What did she look like? Where's home?"

"With the gods."

"That's not possible," Ethan said. "The Greek gods are gone. Long gone."

"Maybe they are but maybe they aren't," Tyler said with a glint in his eye. "Think about it. So much weirdness has happened, I wouldn't be surprised if Zeus climbed through the window and asked us for directions to the nearest ambrosia dealer."

Juniper's words began to slur. "The gods exist in . . . another dimension."

Huh?

"There are only three spatial dimensions," Ethan said, trying to be logical, as usual. "Up and down, left and right, or forward and backward."

"What about special relativity?" Tyler said.

"You can't forget that. Space-time can be thought of as a fourth dimension. And then there's super-string theory, which adds six more dimensions."

My head was starting to spin. "Guys!" I blurted. "Can you please focus? Great-Aunt Juniper, how do we . . . ?" She'd drifted into a deep sleep. "Crud!"

Tyler, Ethan, and I stared at the woman who'd dragged us into this whole mess. Then I sank into a chair. I tried desperately to wrap my head around the situation. "Okay, let's figure this out. Juniper went to the Museum of Fine Arts and tried to tamper with the security system. We don't know why. But she had the urn of Hope with her, in her purse, and it ended up here, in this room. Then a girl came and took it. We don't know who she is or where she went. And some guy has the urn of Faith and used it to rob a bank." I sank deeper into the chair. "What are we supposed to do now?"

As if on cue, the door opened and Louis, the male nurse, stepped in. "Hey, you kids aren't supposed to be in here." He perched his hands on his hips. "This room is off-limits, didn't you read the sign?"

I jumped to my feet. "Sign?" I asked innocently.

He pulled a phone from his pocket. "Do you know Jane Doe? Did you come here to identify her? 'Cause if you did I'm supposed to call the police so they can interview you."

"We don't know her," I said.

"And she doesn't know us," Tyler added. Ethan pulled his baseball cap lower.

"Well, you'll have to leave." Louis stepped aside and motioned toward the hallway. "I don't know how you kids keep getting in here. We need a better security system, that's for sure. I think that other kid climbed in through the window."

"Other kid?" we all said.

"Yeah. I told her she had no business in this room."

"What did she look like?" I asked.

Louis folded his arms. "Why do you want to know what she looks like?"

"Just curious," I told him, because I couldn't think of anything else.

"Only thing I remember is her red hair. Lots of braids, you know."

"Lots of braids?" I froze. No way. That would be weird. It couldn't be . . . *her.*

"She asked me how to get to some sort of comic-book festival. I told her I wasn't a tour guide. If she wanted to get downtown, she could take herself outside and catch the bus."

"When did this happen?" I asked.

"Just a few minutes ago. . . ."

I was out the door, running down the hallway, Ethan and Tyler at my heels.

"Hey," Herman Hofstedder hollered from his wheelchair. "Don't leave me here. Take me with you!"

I darted around a couple more wheelchairs and a lady using a walker. I almost overturned a medication cart. "No running," Sister Beatrice called as I raced by.

"Sorry," I said, then I pushed open the front door. Red braids. Lots of them.

The sound of screeching brakes caught my attention. A city bus had pulled up to the curb, across the street.

"Hey, wait!" I called, waving my arms. "Hold that bus!" But the driver either didn't see me or didn't care, and he began to pull away.

That's when I saw a girl walking down the bus's aisle. She took a seat but she didn't look our way.

She didn't need to. Even through the window-pane, her hair sparkled.

13
ETHAN

FACT: *During a stroke, blood supply is cut off to a portion of the brain. Thus, that portion of the brain stops working correctly, which explains why Great-Aunt Juniper was having hallucinations. The girl hadn't come from the Realm of the Gods. No way.*

"This is insane!" Jax sat in the front seat of Tyler's car as he drove away from Sisters of Mercy. We were following the bus.

I sneezed three times in a row. "Why'd you park under those trees? The car's covered with pollen. It's getting in through the vents." I sneezed again.

"For your information, little brother, I don't choose parking spots based on your overactive immune system."

"Go faster!" Jax ordered in her bossiest voice. "We're gonna lose her."

"Not too fast," I said. "I'd like to remind you of my previously mentioned fact about teenage driving."

"I'd like to remind *both of you* that this is *my* car so *I* will make the driving decisions," Tyler snapped.

A half block away, the bus stopped, its door opened, but the girl didn't get out. Jax wiggled on the seat.

"Is your butt on fire?" Tyler asked.

"No."

"Then stop squirming so much. You're getting on my nerves."

Jax ignored him and kept wiggling. "Go around that taxi," she said as the bus pulled ahead. "Watch out for that bicycle."

"*Don't* tell me how to drive," Tyler grumbled. "Or I will pull over and you can walk." He sounded like Mom. Leaving us at the side of the road was a common threat whenever Tyler and I started to argue in the car. Or whenever I pointed out a rule of the road that Mom was ignoring. Like forgetting her turn signal.

Or not coming to a *complete* stop at an intersection.

Jax turned around and stared at me over the seat back, wide-eyed. "Yesterday, that girl was in Chatham, having gelato with us. Why would she come here and take Juniper's urn?"

"We don't know for sure that she took it," I said. "We saw her on a bus. We never saw her inside Sisters of Mercy."

"Are you serious? The nurse said that a girl with lots of braids was in Juniper's room. And Juniper said she gave the urn to a girl. You think it's just a coincidence that our girl happened to be riding a bus past the Sisters of Mercy at the same time?"

"Okay, so that does sound far-fetched," I said.

"It's obvious what's going on," Tyler said. "She followed me. She's my stalker."

Jax rolled her eyes. "Come on, Tyler. Seriously?"

"I'm a champion. It makes sense I'd have a stalker." He ran a hand over his hair. "I'm smart. I'm charming. She's a superfan. When she sees me in my originally designed costume from Cyclopsville, she'll need a defibrillator."

"Oh really?" Jax said. "And is that why she ran out of the Chatham Creamery? Because you were too much for her heart to handle?"

"Maybe."

"The girl arrived at Sisters of Mercy before us, and she left before us," I pointed out. "That doesn't sound like stalking to me. I think she was trying to avoid us."

Jax whipped around and pointed. "Hurry, the bus is turning right!" Tyler veered into the next lane. If I hadn't been wearing a seat belt I would have been thrown against the door. "Why would she take the urn?" Jax asked, bracing herself as Tyler took a sharp turn. "Who is she?"

For a moment, no one said anything. Then Jax broke the silence. "Do you think she's working for the Camels?"

"It's a possibility," I said. That made a lot more sense than Tyler's theory that she was stalking him, or Juniper's delusion that she was visiting from the Realm of the Gods.

"Remember at the Creamery, how she was asking lots of questions about our aunt? I thought she was being snoopy. I should have told her to mind her own business!" Jax was getting so worked up, she started bouncing. Fortunately, the seat belt kept her from bumping her head on the car's ceiling. "What if the Camels sent her to Chatham to find us? The

Camels know where we live. They know what we look like. What if she went to Merlin's Comics because she wanted to talk to us and find out if we knew where Juniper was hiding? And then we told her. Crud! We fell right into her trap!"

"Are you saying she's not into me?" Tyler asked. "Did you *see* the way she kissed me?"

"Tyler, could you focus on the urn and not on your love life?" Jax pleaded. "We have a serious situation here."

"Well then, explain this." He took another sharp turn, following the bus. "If she's *not* into me, then why did she ask the nurse about the comic-book festival? Huh? Why would she want to go to the festival if not to see me? I invited her, remember?"

"She might want more information," Jax said.

"Or she *might* be into him," I added. It was a possibility. A long shot, but stranger things had happened—like a tornado flying out of an urn.

We followed the bus to Boston Harbor. A sign on a hotel read, *Welcome, International Comic Book Festival Attendees*. "This place looks like it's been invaded by aliens," Jax said. Everyone walking down the street was dressed in a bizarre costume. I recognized some of the characters from classic comic books, like

Superman, Batman, and Wonder Woman. Lots of girls had dyed their hair blue or pink and wore tails. There were pirates and monsters, and all sorts of hats with ears. We drove past a girl in a bikini who'd painted her skin orange.

Tyler rolled down the window. "That's awesome," he called to the orange girl.

The bus stopped near the Seaport World Trade Center. It was flanked on one side by a cruise ship, the *Spirit of Boston*, and on the other side by the Boston Fish Pier and a fleet of colorful fishing boats. "There she is!" Jax exclaimed. The girl stepped off the bus, a tan leather bag hanging from her shoulder.

"Hey!" Tyler hollered out the window. She didn't turn around. His voice wasn't loud enough to cut through all the traffic noise. His voice . . .

"Wait!" I said, before Tyler could holler again. "I figured it out!"

"Figured what out?" Jax asked.

"Her voice. It's been bugging me. She sounds like another voice I'd heard and I just remembered who it is." I swallowed hard. "She has the same accent as the man who hired the Camels. Ricardo."

Jax gasped. "You're right."

Ricardo was a mysterious man who'd hired Mr. and

Mrs. Camel to find the urn. Jax and I had heard his voice over a phone speaker when we'd been hiding in the Camels' motel room. Along with his odd accent, he'd sounded like a classic movie villain—sinister and cold. But we knew nothing more about him. Only that he was still out there, and that he wanted the urn.

"The Camels are in jail," Jax said. "But Ricardo could be anywhere. He could even be here, in Boston. Maybe she works for *him*? We've got to get that urn before he gets it!"

A line had formed outside the center's main entrance. The girl walked to the end of the line and waited. "Pull over," Jax told Tyler.

"What are you going to do?" he asked.

Jax laid out a plan. "She doesn't know that we know she has the urn. Right?" Tyler and I both nodded. "She doesn't know we saw her at Sisters of Mercy and that we followed her here. So, we will pretend to be festival geeks. We'll sneak up on her and grab the urn. You brought costumes, right?"

"Of course. It's a comic-book festival." Tyler pulled into a load/unload zone, got out, and opened the trunk. "Here," he said, handing Jax a black cape and a stretchy black mask.

"Perfect," Jax said. She fixed the cape around her shoulders. The mask covered her head and half her face, with two holes for her eyes, and two pointy ears at the very top. "Shouldn't I have a tail?"

"Why?" Tyler asked.

"Because I'm Catwoman."

Tyler rolled his eyes. "Have you been living in a cave or something? You're not Catwoman. You're Batgirl."

"What's the difference?"

"What's the difference?" Tyler's voice rose an octave. "Seriously? One's *a bat*. One's *a cat*."

"Why do you have to be so snippy all the time?" Jax pulled her mask into place.

I looked down the sidewalk. More people had joined the end of the line. "The line's moving," I said. Jax grabbed another cape out of the trunk and handed it to me. "No way," I told her. "I hate costumes."

"Ethan, I need your help. I can't touch the urn or I'll get those weird feelings again. So I'll distract her and you'll grab the bag."

"Me? Grab the bag?" I frowned. "Have Tyler do it."

"Tyler has to stay out here because we're gonna need a getaway car." Jax tied the cape around my neck. Mine was solid black, while Jax's had a yellow lining. "Don't worry. You'll make an excellent sidekick."

"Actually," Tyler said, "Ethan's not the sidekick. He's wearing the Batman cape. That makes *you* the sidekick."

"Why is Batgirl the sidekick?" Jax whined. "Just because she's a girl?"

"No, because Batman reigns supreme in the bat universe. He's the nucleus and everyone else revolves around him." Tyler handed me a mask.

I'd never been the nucleus before. With great trepidation, I took off my baseball cap and pulled the mask over my face. I thought about what the latex might do to my skin. There'd be no circulation. Latex was a common allergen. Would I break out in hives?

Tyler tossed my cap into the trunk. Then he faced us, his arms folded. "Look, as much as I don't want to get anywhere near that urn, I agree that we have to get it back. But if something goes wrong, and she opens it—"

"She's not going to open it. We're going to sneak up on her," Jax said.

"But if she does open it, you'll both be attacked. Do you understand what that means?"

"We'll turn into zombies," Jax said.

"Uh, not *technically* zombies," I corrected, my stomach clenching.

Tyler frowned. "Mom would kill me if she knew I let you guys go after this thing. I'm the oldest. I should go."

"We need you to drive," Jax reminded him. "Besides, you were the hero last time, Tyler. Now it's our turn."

Being a hero didn't matter to me. I wished I had my driver's license.

"I'll circle the block," Tyler said. "Call me as soon as you have it and I'll bring the car right back here, to this spot."

"Then what?" I asked, my face already starting to sweat.

"I have no idea," Jax said. "But we'll figure it out. You ready to do this, Batman?"

I felt like we were about to jump off a bridge without a bungee cord. I tugged on my mask. "No."

She smiled. "That's the spirit. Let's go get our hope-sucking urn back."

We hurried toward the conference center, capes flapping. Tyler's gaming music would have been the perfect accompaniment. Even though everyone else was in costume, I still felt like a freak. Luckily, no one could see my face.

A slight breeze blew off the harbor, but I was already hot and miserable. It felt like I'd pulled a pair of tights over my face. We took our place at the end of the line. Twenty people stood between us and the girl. There was another Batman, a pair of ninjas, a bunch of Star Wars characters, and a little kid in a panda suit. I stood real close to Jax, my arm pressing against hers. It was too muggy to stand so close but Jax didn't step away. I needed to feel her arm, to know that I wasn't alone among all these strangers.

We watched the girl. If Jax's eyes had been lasers they would have burned a hole in her back.

"Why don't we go up and ask her to give us the urn?" I suggested. "She seemed very nice at the Creamery. She might give it back."

"Or she might open it and use it against us," Jax said.

I didn't argue with that logic. I knew we were both remembering the sound of Tyler's agonizing scream, and the way his body had fallen to the ground like an empty sack. How he'd stared into space, lost in his own emptiness. I tried to push those thoughts away because they were making my legs tremble.

"We'll follow her and snatch the bag when she's distracted," Jax said.

I hoped the girl hadn't studied karate or any other form of martial arts.

Fifteen minutes later she reached the security gate. The officer opened her leather bag and looked inside. My whole body stiffened. What if the guard pulled out the urn? Could we run fast enough to get to the front of the line and grab it out of the guard's hands? I clenched my toes, ready to sprint. But the guard closed the bag, then said, "Okay, go in." She slung the bag over her shoulder and headed into the trade center. One minute later, we were through security.

I don't remember the next five minutes.

14
JAX

The lobby was blindingly bright, thanks to the giant chandeliers. And it was jam-packed with people, some lined up at registration tables, some hanging out and talking to friends. A giant reader board was set on an easel and read, *International Comic Book Festival.* A voice over a loudspeaker gave directions to the exhibition hall.

As I pushed between people, I caught a glimpse of the girl. She was clearly on a mission. She marched right past a lady who was handing out free smoothies. How can you ignore a free smoothie?

"There she goes," I said. I was going to jab Ethan with my elbow but he wasn't next to me. "Ethan?"

Even though it was crowded, I was surprised that I'd lost him so quickly. A bunch of other black capes caught my eye until I landed on his. He stood in a corner, next to an escalator, his bat ears blending into the shadows. For a moment I forgot about the urn. Ethan needed me.

I shoved my way through a pack of wookies to get to him. He'd wedged himself into a safe little nook, like a bat might do. "Ethan?" I said.

He covered his real ears, not his bat ears. "It's loud."

"It is loud," I agreed. Background music mixed with chattering voices. Constant announcements blasted from the PA system. It was super crowded *and* super loud—a combination that always freaked Ethan out. He'd tried to explain it to me. He'd said that all the noises got jumbled up into one big ball of noise, and it made his head hurt.

"I'm here," I said, taking his hand. He opened his eyes and stared down at his sneakers. It often took a few minutes to snap him out of this daze. "Come on," I told him. Then I gently led him to a water fountain.

"But . . ." He frowned.

"Don't worry about germs. Just take a drink.

It will make you feel better." I glanced over my shoulder. I couldn't see the girl.

Ethan drank. "Feel better?" I asked. He looked really odd with that mask on. But even if he'd been in a lineup with a bunch of other guys in masks, I'd know Ethan's eyes because they were gentle. And kind.

"Guess I'm better as a sidekick," he said.

"That's not true." Okay, maybe it was true but at least he was talking. "Do you need to stay here until you feel better? Or can you come with me?"

"You can't do this alone," he said. "You can't touch the urn, remember?" I wanted to hug him right then, because I knew he'd rather sit in the corner, unnoticed. Or go back outside, where the steady thrum of traffic would be a relief from the convention center's clatter. Ethan was a pain sometimes, with his allergies, his nosebleeds, and his shyness. But then he'd surprise me and face his fears. He was a lot stronger than he looked.

We headed into the main exhibition hall. It was the size of a football field. Rows of booths, separated by wide aisles, ran the length of the room.

I found her right away. She was walking quickly down the first aisle, looking from side to side. The place was packed. I crinkled my nose. Even though the room was air-conditioned, there were lots of heavy, furry costumes, so the BO factor was pretty strong.

"What's the plan?" Ethan asked.

I started to form one on the spot. "I'll bump into her, then while I'm apologizing, you'll grab her bag and disappear into the crowd." The same thoughts repeated over and over in my head. Who was she? Had someone paid her to get the urn? But the most important question at that moment was, Could Ethan outrun her? Her legs were longer than his. Maybe I could trip her, to give Ethan a head start.

"Hey," I said, as a big guy stepped on my foot. I tried to slip around him but his friends got in the way. They wore plastic armor, ridges on their foreheads, and fake beards. The guy said something to me in a weird language, then grunted. They all grunted, and beat their chests. "What's your problem?" I asked, trying to squeeze between them. I'd lost sight of the Greek girl.

They laughed, said more stuff I didn't understand, but the tone made me think it wasn't very nice. Then, after another round of grunts, they let me pass.

"They're jerks," I said to Ethan.

"Actually, they're Klingons," he explained. "I think they were speaking Klingon."

Yeesh. Those *Star Trek* geeks took their role-playing way too seriously. "Hey, where is she?" I forgot all about the rude Trekkies. Where was the girl? My heart jumped into my throat. Had we lost her? I pushed between two ninja turtles. "Get your big green torsos out of my way!"

"Hey, Batgirl, watch where you're going," one of them snarled.

Maybe I was being rude with all the pushing but I didn't care. Some things were more important than manners. Like saving the world from being zombiefied.

I reached the end of the aisle, turned the corner, then hurried up the next aisle. More booths, more people, but no girl with sparkly red braids. I felt like screaming. I felt like going back and kicking those stupid Klingons in their hairy shins!

An announcement filled the hall. "Elvish Language Workshop will begin in ten minutes in Plaza A. Also, tickets are still available for tonight's Steampunk Ball in the Plaza Ballroom."

"Ethan, where is she?" I was seriously starting to panic. "Do you see her?" My eyes zipped back and forth as I wove around princesses, aliens, and galactic soldiers. Then, just as tears began to sting my eyes, she appeared. I don't think she noticed us in our bat costumes, because as she hurried past, her leather bag brushed against my arm.

The urn. I felt it.

It was a sensation I'd longed to forget. Immediately, like a mother whose child has gone missing, I needed to hold the urn, to protect it from the rest of the world. I could feel it calling to me, pulling me like a moth to light.

I am the protector of the urn.

I broke out in a cold sweat. There was no doubt about it. The urn of Hope was here, at the festival. She'd taken it from Great-Aunt Juniper!

Then the girl stopped in her tracks, spun around, and looked right into my bat eyes. "Go home, Jax. This is too dangerous for you."

I didn't know what to say.

First—how had she recognized me? I had a black latex mask pulled over my head!

Second—I wanted that urn!

Ethan stood beside me. His gaze moved quickly between my face and hers. I didn't tell him that I'd felt the urn when the bag brushed against me.

I didn't tell him that I was scared. Last month, I'd carried that urn in my arms, I'd even slept beside it, not knowing what it could do to a person's soul. But now I knew. I knew that if she wanted, she could open her bag, uncork the urn, and in an instant, everyone in the hall would collapse to the ground, including me and Ethan. Darkness would overtake us, drowning us in sadness. I took a long breath, trying to steady my trembling legs. The urge overtook me and . . .

I grabbed the bag!

The tug of war lasted about one second. She was way stronger. "Go home," she repeated, hugging the bag to her chest.

The Batgirl mask suddenly felt suffocating so I yanked it off. I didn't need to hide my face any longer. My hair was plastered to my forehead with sweat. "You stole the urn from our great-aunt. I am its protector. Give it back!"

She frowned. "You are mistaken. I did not steal the urn. Your great-aunt gave it to me willingly."

What a total liar! "She gave it to you because she's confused. She thought you were . . ." It sounded so crazy.

Ethan took off his Batman mask. His face was

so red and shiny, it looked like he might be getting a rash. I thought he was going to say something, but he reached into his pocket and pulled out his phone, which was ringing. "Hello?"

Even though the conference floor was loud, Tyler's voice boomed out of the speaker. "What's going on in there? I've circled the block a dozen times. Do you have the freakin' urn or what?"

"We're talking to her now," Ethan said.

I stepped between the girl and Ethan, summoning every ounce of courage I could find. As long as I didn't touch the bag again, the weird feelings would go away. The urn had taken over my mind in Washington, DC, and I'd thought that everyone in the world was going to steal the urn. I'd tried to sneak away from Ethan and Tyler. I'd tried to keep the urn for myself. But this time I would be more careful.

"Look, I know you have it," I told her, keeping my arms at my sides. "But why did you bring it here? Are you meeting someone? Is someone paying you?"

She glanced around. Who was she looking for?

"If you give it back to us right now, we won't call the police." Of course we'd never call police.

The last thing we needed was for the urn to be taken into custody as evidence or worse—uncorked because they thought it contained drugs.

She didn't flinch. She looked me right in the eye. "Do not interfere with my quest, Jax Malone. Return to your home before you get hurt." It didn't sound like a threat. It sounded like she actually cared about my safety. She turned and continued up the aisle, the bag slung, once again, over her shoulder.

I groaned with frustration. She'd called my bluff. All I could do was hurry after her, Ethan at my heels.

Then she stopped in front of a booth. Its banner read, *The Puzzle Master.*

"Hey," Ethan said. "Tyler mentioned this, remember? He told her to visit this booth if she came to the festival."

I nodded. But why, after stealing a magical urn, would she stop here?

The shelves were filled with board games and jigsaw puzzles. People stood around a table, working on different puzzles, some wooden, some made from metal. Rubik's Cubes were stacked to the ceiling.

"Are you the puzzle master?" the girl asked a woman who was sitting on a stool. The woman was very plump, with frizzy black hair sticking out of a red scarf. Her big, golden hoop earrings and white blouse made her look like a pirate wench.

"The one and only," the woman said.

"It was told to me that you are an expert in puzzles."

"That's true." Then she pointed at a little boy. "Hey, kid! Don't open the box unless you're going to buy it!" The boy put the box down and darted away.

Ethan and I stood to the side, watching as the girl reached into her black bag and pulled out a brown leather belt. She straightened the leather belt and held it in front of the woman. The puzzle master pursed her lips. "I don't sell belts," she said. "Costumes are in aisle five." The girl flipped the belt over and the puzzle master's eyes widened. "Oh, I see." She leaned close to the leather. "What language is this?"

"Greek," the girl answered.

"I'm afraid I don't read Greek."

"I do, but this message makes no sense. The letters form no words."

The puzzle master tapped a finger to her round chin. "It would appear that what you have is a cipher."

"A cipher?"

"Indeed. A cipher is like a code, however it requires a key. Let me show you." The puzzle master slid off her stool, then pulled a box from one of her shelves. After opening the box, she removed a wooden rod and a long strip of leather. Ethan and I stepped closer so we could see what was going on. "When ancient armies needed to communicate, they often used a cipher. The commanders would carry identical rods. After winding the leather around the rod, a message was written along the length of the leather. You see how it says, The enemy is near?"

The girl nodded. So did Ethan and I.

The puzzle master continued. "Once the message was written, the leather strip was unwound and the blank spaces filled in with other letters. Thus, when the leather strip lies flat, the message is indecipherable to the naked eye." She unwound the leather and showed it to the girl.

"It makes no sense," the girl said.

"Exactly. That is the genius of a cipher. Only

those with the proper key can *decipher* the message." She rewound the leather onto the rod. "*Voilà*. The message appears once again."

The girl took her leather belt and began to wind it around the wooden rod. "It doesn't fit," she said.

"It will only work if you find the correct size key, both in length and width."

"What does this have to do with the urn?" I asked Ethan. We were standing shoulder to shoulder, watching as the girl tucked the belt back into her bag.

"I don't know," he said, reaching into his pocket. His phone was ringing again.

"Tell Tyler to quit calling. We're trying to accomplish something!" Seriously, Tyler had zero patience. All he had to do was wait in the car and be ready to drive at warp speed. We were doing all the work. But how were we supposed to focus when he kept interrupting?

But Ethan pushed the telephone in front of my face. The screen read, *Ricardo*.

15
ETHAN

FACT: *There are two types of stress—acute and chronic. My nosebleeds came from acute stress, which is a temporary reaction to a situation or event—like lying to my parents or getting a phone call from a mysterious evil villain. Chronic means living in a constant state of stress. I was heading in that direction, thanks to the urn situation.*

The tickle in my sinuses began the instant I read the screen.

Incoming Call from Ricardo.

I didn't wonder how he'd gotten my number. So

many people assume we still have privacy. That is an illusion. Any time you do anything online, or by phone, you make yourself traceable, trackable, contactable. What I was trying to figure out was— should I accept or decline?

It rang again.

"Don't answer it," Jax said. She shuffled in place. "I mean, why would we answer it? We don't want to talk to *him*. Then again, maybe we should answer it. Would it hurt to answer? I don't know what to do." She looked at me, her face all scrunched up as if she was about to get sick.

"If I answer the call, he'll hear exactly where we are," I said. "Although there's also a GPS tracking unit in my phone."

"What? Why do you have one of those things?"

"They come with the phone," I told her.

"Then *don't* answer it."

The phone stopped ringing. We both gasped as a message popped onto the screen. From Ricardo: *We must talk about the urn. Meet me at the concession stand. Now.*

"He's here?" Jax cried.

I pinched the bridge of my nose. The tingling was stronger now. The bleeding would start soon.

"I knew it!" Jax said. "She came here to meet him. She's working for him. If we don't get that urn, she's going to give it to him."

"If she's going to meet him, then why is he calling us?" I asked, pulling a wad of Kleenex from my pocket.

"I don't know. This whole thing is crazy." Jax whipped around. "Ethan? Where did she go?"

The girl was no longer in the Puzzle Master's booth.

"Do you see her?" Jax asked. We hurried down the aisle. "She could have reached the exit already."

"But Ricardo's at the concession stand. Wouldn't she go there?" I held the tissues to my nose.

"Concession stand! Of course!" Jax led the way down the aisle. "This is a really bad time for a nosebleed, Ethan."

"There's no need to point out the obvious." I checked the tissues. Phew! There was no blood. I'd applied enough pressure. "Are we really doing this? Are we really going to meet Ricardo?" I asked.

"What other choice do we have?"

I started to list a half dozen other choices, but Jax was too far ahead of me to hear any of them.

The concession stand was actually a bunch of different vendors whose booths were lined up along the back wall. The scent of fast food filled the air.

Every table was crowded, the conversation level high. A group of Pokémon characters sat eating mini pizzas. The Fabulous Four were slurping noodles. Jax ducked behind a display of energy drinks that had been stacked like a pyramid. "Put the mask back on," she said.

As much as I dreaded the mask, I pulled it over my face. Ricardo probably knew exactly what we looked like, thanks to the Camels. If he'd been following us, then he also knew what we looked like in our bat costumes. Hiding seemed impossible.

I imagined what would happen if Ricardo opened the urn. It would be like a scene from a comic book. The tornado would whip through the hall, churning up everything in its path. Characters would fall to the floor, waiting for someone to save them. As the urn took all the hope it could find, Ricardo would laugh wickedly. Batman and Batgirl would be powerless to help. We'd be stupefied like everyone else.

"Do you see her?" Jax asked.

"No." And since we didn't know what Ricardo looked like, I didn't see him, either.

"Call Tyler. Warn him that the girl might be leaving the building. Tell him to follow her, even if he has to leave without us."

I unlocked my phone and was about to press

Tyler's number, when it rang again. *Incoming Call from Ricardo.* Jax grabbed it and pressed *Accept.* Then she pressed *Speaker.* "Leave us alone. We don't have the urn!"

"Hello, Jacqueline. There is no reason to be afraid of me. I am here to help you." His voice was exactly as I remembered from when we hid in the Camels' hotel bathroom. It gave me the chills then, and still did. He sounded like he could turn things to ice. "You are in great danger. You must give me the urn."

"Why are we in danger?"

"The urn will hurt you, as it hurt your cousin. Give it to me and I will destroy it."

He wanted to destroy it? I looked at Jax. Maybe he wasn't a bad guy after all. Maybe he was on our side. But Jax narrowed her eyes with suspicion. "We don't have it."

"That is a lie," he hissed. "You will not leave the Seaport World Trade Center until you give me the urn."

"I don't know what you're talking about." Jax was trying to sound calm but her voice was trembling. "We're not at the Seaport whatever-you-just-called-it."

"Do not play games with me, Jacqueline Malone. I followed you here. I know you have the urn because I can sense its presence. It is close. Very close. You will surrender or face the consequences."

"We're not afraid of you!" Jax said, then she hung up.

"Jax?" My voice cracked. The tingling was peaking, and the nosebleed would start any second now. I grabbed her arm and pointed.

A man was walking toward us, a phone held in one hand. He was tall and skinny, wearing black pants, a black shirt, and a black fedora. His stride was fast and determined. He pushed a little girl out of his way.

"Run!" Jax said.

We turned on our heels and headed in the opposite direction. Once again, there was no plan. How could we have a plan? None of this made sense. If the girl was delivering the urn to Ricardo, then he'd know she had it. But he thought *we* had it. He'd followed us. He knew we were visiting Juniper. He—

Something crashed behind us. I looked over my shoulder. The tower of energy drinks tumbled to the floor, the bottles rolling in all directions. Neither Jax nor I had bumped into it, so why had it fallen over? Ricardo stumbled.

"Keep running!" a voice ordered. A shape darted in front of me. Red braids swung back and forth as the girl grabbed a stack of folding chairs and threw them to the ground behind us. Like a bulldozer, she pushed though the crowd. She knocked into a kid carrying an armful of books. When she grabbed a stand of toy swords and tossed it behind us, I realized she was creating the obstacle course on purpose. I might have pointed out that she was engaging in vandalism, but this was one occasion when breaking the law was okay by me. She raced in front of Jax and motioned for us to follow. Was she leading us *away* from Ricardo?

What was going on? Who was the good guy and who was the bad guy?

Our capes flying, Jax and I tore after her. I glanced back again. We'd gained some ground. Ricardo was caught in the sword chaos, as people rushed to the scene trying to help clean the mess. It suddenly looked like we might outrun him. But another problem reared its head—we'd attracted the attention of three security guards. As we dashed out of the exhibition hall and past the registration tables, the guards joined the chase. "Stop!" one of them called. The entrance wasn't far. Only a few more yards to run and a group of Klingons to get past.

I squeezed between plastic armored chests and fake battle weapons. Jax stopped and said something to the biggest one, a guy who must have been three hundred pounds. He growled and said something in the language of his people. The next thing I knew, they were stomping away, like an army on the warpath. The entrance was free and clear. I turned again, catching sight of the Klingons blocking Ricardo's path. They were waving their arms and jumping up and down.

"What did you say to them?" I asked Jax.

"I told them that the man chasing us was Spock in disguise."

Brilliant, I thought.

The girl raced toward the exit and out she went, her braids swaying with her long strides. Jax was next. As I emerged from the convention hall, a soft breeze brushed across my face, carrying the scent of seawater. Immediate relief washed over me. No elbow-to-elbow crowd. No loud music, no blaring announcements. Cars drove past. A boat honked in the harbor. Would life return to normal?

But what was that screeching sound?

It was like a James Bond movie. Pedestrians jumped aside as Tyler's car skidded to a stop right in front of us. Huh? I looked around. This wasn't a road. He'd driven onto the sidewalk. That wasn't legal! Mom would kill him!

The girl grabbed the front passenger door and

yanked it open. Then she flung herself inside. Jax opened the back and dove in. I looked over my shoulder. Through the glass entryway doors I could see a tall, dark figure rushing down the hallway. And three security guards.

"Ethan!" Jax cried.

I scrambled in next to her and slammed the door shut.

"Well, hello there," Tyler said to the girl. "This is unexpected. Did you come back to see me?" He smiled.

"No time to talk," Jax said. She and I were breathing like out-of-shape racehorses. "Ricardo is chasing us!"

"There he is!" I announced as Ricardo burst out of the building, the guards on his tail.

"I advise you to move your chariot," the girl told Tyler.

"Go, go, go!" Jax hollered.

Tires screeched as Tyler did a 180-degree turn. A car horn blared as we bounced over the curb and pulled onto the road. To avoid a head-on collision, Tyler slammed the brakes. Jax and I were thrown against the front seat. Another car honked. We desperately searched for the seat belts. Just as we strapped in, Tyler accelerated and we were thrown backward. "You're going to get us killed," Jax complained, rubbing the back of her neck.

"Don't tell the getaway driver how to drive," he snapped.

I guessed that it wasn't the appropriate time to remind them, once again, about the dangers of teenage driving.

Both Jax and I looked out the back window. Ricardo stood on the sidewalk, his face clenched as if he was about to have a heart attack. I'd never seen anyone look so angry. He yanked his phone from his pocket. Ringing filled Tyler's car. My phone's screen glowed. *Incoming Call: Ricardo.* "He's trying to track us!" Jax cried. "Don't answer it!"

As blood trickled from my left nostril, I opened my privacy settings and disabled the GPS tracking device. Then I muted the phone. "He can't track us now."

Jax tore off her mask and fell against the seat. "That was so close. He almost caught us."

I struggled to get my mask off. As I pushed a wad of tissue against my nostril, Jax cringed. She's always gagged at the sight of blood. It was one of the few things that grossed her out. "You broke a lot of stuff," I told the girl. "We could get in serious trouble. What if the security guards take down our license plate number and call the police?" As I tilted my head back, I imagined Mom and Dad getting a phone call from the festival organizers, or from the Boston police chief. I'd promised I wouldn't let Jax get me into any more trouble.

"Somebody better tell me what's going on," Tyler said. "Where's the urn?"

Jax leaned over the seat and pointed at the girl's leather bag.

Tyler gripped the steering wheel, his knuckles turning white. The road led us over a bridge. Boston Harbor lay on our right, a channel on our left. He glanced nervously at the girl, who was hugging her bag to her chest. "I don't want that urn in my car. I don't want to be anywhere near it," he said through clenched teeth.

I didn't want to be near the urn, either. But our goal was to keep it away from people like Ricardo. I looked at Jax. She was deep in thought, her eyes narrowed, probably planning her next move.

"The urn will not harm you," the girl said, wrapping her arms tighter. "Do not try to take it from me."

Jax and I looked at each other. Was the urn having the same effect on the girl as it had on Jax? Did she think of herself as the protector? Would she do anything to keep it safe?

"Listen," Jax told her. "That urn makes you feel weird. It gets into your head. It will tell you to protect it. It'll make you think that we're bad, but we're not bad. We want to do the right thing."

"And what is the right thing?" She turned halfway around. Her hair sparkled in the sunlight that streamed through the windshield.

"We want to give it back to our great-aunt," Jax said. "It belongs to her. She is the rightful owner."

The girl's voice remained calm. "That is incorrect. I am the rightful owner."

Despite my nosebleed, I kept looking back, to see if anyone was following. So far, it looked like we were safe. "Where are we going?" I asked.

"I have no idea," Tyler admitted. He followed the road to the right. The harbor was still in view and we passed a sign for an aquarium.

"You are taking me to Poseidon," the girl said as she looked out the passenger window.

"Huh?" Tyler asked "Where?"

"There is a fountain nearby, in which Poseidon is seated. I must return to that place immediately. My quest is to return the urns."

Jax gasped. "Did you say urns? As in more than one?"

Tyler smiled. "Did you say *quest*? As in 'a hero's journey'?" It was one of his favorite words. Almost equal to "trophy."

The girl didn't answer, just kept looking out the window. When Tyler slowed down for a red light, she threw open the passenger door and bolted from the car. "Where are you going?" he called.

"Home," she yelled. She dashed up the sidewalk, then turned into a park.

"Crud," Tyler said with a groan. "I keep forgetting to ask her name."

"Her name?" Jax unbuckled her seat belt and flung herself at my window so she could get a better view. "Who cares about her name? She's got the urn! Pull over!"

Tyler pulled the car to the curb. The girl hurried up to a large fountain, then stood in front of it. "I knew it," Jax said as she unlocked the door. "She's waiting for someone. She's going to hand over the urn. We have to grab it before it's too late."

Tyler shook his head. "No way. I'm not touching it. That thing almost killed me."

"You know I can't touch it. It makes me crazy." Jax reached across my lap and pushed open the door. "Ethan, you have to do it. Hurry."

This seemed ridiculous, at best. Tyler was twice my

size and fueled by caffeine. He could easily overpower the girl. And Jax was twice as fast as me and had one setting—hyper. She could outrun anyone. But they were going to rely on me? We'd already tried tug-of-war with the girl. And lost.

My nose started to tickle again. "But—"

"There's no time for buts," Jax said, which was something Mom often said to me. As did my teachers. Jax started pushing me out of the car. "Same plan as last time. Tyler will man the getaway car, I'll distract, you'll grab."

"Fine," I grumbled under my breath.

Though we were still wearing our capes, at least we'd taken off those suffocating masks. The girl was still standing in front of the fountain as we tiptoed into the park. The fountain's basin was round and filled to the brim with water. Four stone figures sat in the center, water spouting around them. Above the statues was a tier, then above that another tier—like a cake stand set on top of another cake stand.

Her back was to us. I looked around to see if anyone was acting suspiciously. Then I realized that Jax and I were the only two people who were acting suspiciously. I stopped tiptoeing.

Two old ladies sat on a bench, sipping drinks and talking. A kid with a skateboard was tying his shoe.

Another lady was scooping her dog's poop. Ricardo was nowhere to be seen, which was a huge relief.

"I'll grab her around the waist and hold her," Jax said. "You take the urn. Then we run."

"Won't that make us muggers?" I asked, picturing myself in a mug shot. Should I smile at the camera or look serious? Maybe I should have worn a nicer shirt.

"We're not muggers because we're not stealing. We're taking back something that belongs to us. It's totally different." She flexed her fingers, preparing for the tackle. "You ready?"

"Uh, why is she climbing into the fountain?" I asked. "Doesn't she know that's against the rules? The sign says no swimming."

With the leather bag over her shoulder, the girl had stepped into the fountain's basin. The water reached up to her calves. She walked toward the center, then stood in front of one of the statues. She tucked the bag under her arm, touched the statue's head . . .

. . . and disappeared.

"Wait!" Tyler hollered out the car window. "I still don't know your name! What is your name?"

16
JAX

The girl had disappeared right before our eyes.

I gasped so long and so hard, I almost choked on my own spit. "Did you see that?"

Ethan's mouth hung open. If he stood like that for much longer, he'd swallow a bug.

"That did *not* just happen," I said, staring at the empty space where she'd stood. "No, no, no, no, no." I ran around the fountain. Where was she? The two ladies were jabbering away on the bench and the kid on the skateboard had his back turned. "Did you see where that girl went?" I asked the ladies. "Did you see the girl with the red braids?" I asked the skateboarder. They saw nothing. You'd

143

think someone driving past would have noticed a girl disappear into thin air, but maybe everyone was too busy texting and driving to look out the window.

Ethan finally blinked. "I don't believe it."

I stood next to him, panting because I'd run around the fountain like six times. "This just keeps getting weirder and weirder."

And so we waited for her to come back. What else could we do? She had the urn. We wanted the urn.

"How long has it been?" I asked.

Tyler and I were sitting on a bench near the fountain. "Two minutes longer than the last time you asked," he grumbled. It had taken him forever to find a parking space because of the whole parallel parking problem. "I'm starving. I need a sandwich or something."

I was hungry too. We hadn't eaten since that morning and it was almost dinnertime. But hello? We had some serious issues to deal with. And Ricardo could call at any moment. "Tyler, stop thinking about food and focus. We have a lot of questions to answer. First of all, we need to figure out where she went."

"She said she was going home."

"Home? She walked into a fountain, Tyler. That's not home."

He leaned back on the bench, stretching his legs. "She told Great-Aunt Juniper that she was from the Realm of the Gods, right? So maybe that's where she went."

I rolled my eyes. "You're kidding, right?"

"Negatory, little cousin. I am presenting the possibility that she traveled to another dimension." He said it like it made sense. "Check Google Maps for Realm of the Gods and get me some directions." I expected him to laugh but he didn't. "I'm not kidding. Check."

"That's idiotic," Ethan said. He'd been mostly silent since the disappearance. I'm sure he was trying to figure out a rational explanation. I was hoping he'd come up with one because, even though I already believed some pretty wacky things, I wasn't ready to believe that the girl had traveled to *another dimension*.

"Fine. I'll do it." While Tyler searched his phone, Ethan started walking around the fountain, looking for trapdoors, or escape hatches, or anything physical that might explain what we saw. "Maybe it was an illusion," he said. "Like when we went to that magic show and found that hole in the stage." I'd talked him into sneaking backstage after the show, without permission. I'd ended up grounded, but at least I'd figured out how a magician's assistant could "disappear" in the blink of an eye.

"Nothing," Tyler reported. "Not even a street view." His stomach growled, which made mine growl, as if they were talking to each other. "I'd eat my own sock if I had some ketchup," he said. I was starting to think that Tyler's brain shut down when he was hungry. Street view? Hello?

I darted to my feet. "Maybe we can figure it out if we reenact the moment. I'm going to stand exactly where she was standing." I took off my shoes, rolled up my pant legs, and climbed in. Ethan immediately rushed to the side of the fountain. "I know, I know, the sign says no swimming. I'm researching."

He frowned. "The water looks filthy."

It did. The color probably came from pigeon poop. "Don't worry. I'm not going to drink it."

As I walked toward the middle, where the statues were posed, I stepped on a few wishing coins. I used to toss coins into fountains when I was little. But Ethan had convinced me that it was a waste of money, because there was no such thing as magic. I smiled, remembering that conversation. Nothing was the same anymore. I wished Great-Aunt Juniper were with us. She'd know what to do.

I stopped in front of a statue, the one with the beard. "She stood here, right?"

"Yes," Ethan said.

I put my hands on my hips and waited. Nothing happened. "What did you find out about this place?" I asked.

Ethan read his phone. "It's called Brewer Fountain. It's made of bronze and was cast in Paris. It was broken for a long time but was recently restored. The building across the way is the Massachusetts State House."

"I'm going to go look for some food and coffee," Tyler hollered. "Who's coming with me?"

"Ethan and I are *doing* something," I hollered back. Then I walked through the water, looking at the statues. There was the bearded man, then a lady, then another man, then another lady. They were all half-naked and sitting.

"If she comes back, will you tell her to wait for me?" Tyler asked. "I don't want to miss her. Do you think she'd go on a date with me?"

I was too busy trying to solve this mystery to worry about Tyler's love life. I looked closely at the statues' faces. "Who are these people?"

"Let's see . . ." Ethan scanned his screen. "Two of them are Acis and Galatea."

Hearing those names, Tyler forgot his hunger, at least for a moment. "Hey, I know all about the story of Acis and Galatea because there's a Cyclops in it." He walked around the perimeter of the fountain and pointed to the younger female figure, whose hair was coiled on top of her head. "That's Galatea. She was a beautiful sea nymph and she was in love with this guy, Acis." He pointed to the younger man. The two statues were gazing at each other. "But there was a Cyclops named Polyphemus who loved Galatea. Polyphemus was a jerk, which is basically the personality description for all Cyclopses. And he had a massive inferiority complex. But he was also a realist. He knew that if Galatea was forced to choose between a handsome man with two eyes or a big ugly brute with one gigantic eye in the middle of his forehead, she'd choose the handsome guy. So Polyphemus went into a jealous rage and smashed Acis to death with a boulder. His guts sprayed all over the place."

"Eeew," I said.

"So much blood poured out of Acis that it turned into a river, which today is named after him. Supposedly, his spirit lives in the water."

The sculptor had given Galatea and Acis expressions of longing. They were seated apart, not touching, just staring at each other for eternity. "What a sad story."

"In Cyclopsville, we created the Cave of Polyphemus on level three. You have to dodge his flying boulders. If you don't . . . BAM! You become a puddle of gelatinous goo, and you have to be reenergized by a team member."

Ethan read his screen again. "The other two figures are Poseidon and Amphitrite."

Tyler walked back around the fountain. "That man with the beard is Poseidon, the Greek god of the sea," he said. Then he pointed to the other woman. "His wife, Amphitrite, was also a sea nymph."

"When the girl disappeared, she was standing in front of Poseidon," I said. "Did she touch anything with her hands?"

"Yes," Ethan said. "She touched the statue's head." I touched the head, but nothing happened. "Maybe there's a release lever under the water," Ethan suggested.

I felt around with my toes. What would I do if I was suddenly transported somewhere? I would *freak out*, no doubt about it. Like when you reach the top of a roller coaster and you're screaming because it's going to be fun *and* terrifying. But my toes found no latches or buttons, just a bunch of coins. I looked at Poseidon's face. "Hello?" I said to him. "Can you hear me?"

"What are you doing?" Ethan asked.

"She's talking to a statue," Tyler told him.

"I can see she's talking to a statue," Ethan grumbled. We were all getting very cranky. Food would be a good thing.

I watched Poseidon's face, half expecting it to start moving, like in the scene from that old movie, *A Christmas Carol*, when Scrooge's lion-faced door knocker starts to talk. That always scared me when I was little. Maybe Poseidon's eyes were a one-way mirror, like the kind they used in police interrogation movies. "Hello?" I leaned closer. "Can you hear me? We want to talk to the girl."

"Young lady?"

You know that expression, "I almost jumped out of my skin?" Well, that's exactly how I felt when that booming voice filled the air. But Poseidon's mouth hadn't moved. I narrowed my eyes. "Are you talking to me?"

"Yes, I'm talking to you."

I whipped around. A Boston police officer stood between Tyler and Ethan. His short-sleeve shirt was tucked into his dark pants, and a silver badge was pinned on the left side. He pointed at a sign. *No playing or swimming in the fountain.* "Don't tell me you can't read."

"Sorry," I said as I climbed out.

"Where are your parents?"

"They're . . . around. They went for a walk." I didn't look away because that's a sure sign of lying. And I didn't reach down to wipe the water droplets that were rolling down my shins. I looked right into his suspicious eyes. Ethan reached up for his baseball cap, to pull it lower like he always did, but it wasn't on his head. He'd left it in the car trunk. His cheeks turned red as the officer checked us out. I'm sure Ethan was worried about lying to a police officer, but what else could we do? We'd end up in the mental ward if we told the real story.

Lucky for us, the officer didn't seem interested in what three kids were doing in the park. "Stay out of the fountain. If I find you in there again, I'll write you a ticket."

"Okay. Thank you," I said. As he walked away, he kept turning to check on us. We all waved innocently.

"That was close," Ethan said after a loud sigh.

"Let's go eat," Tyler said.

I waved at the cop again, smiling like a contestant in a beauty pageant. Then, out of the corner of my mouth, I said, "I'm not leaving until she comes back. She said *urns*, plural. She must know about the other two, so maybe she'll be coming back." I sat on the bench. "I have a feeling about this." It wasn't like a psychic premonition, or a voice in my head. It was a hunch. And I wanted her to come back, because I had a zillion questions.

"I'll get food," Tyler said. "But call me the nanosecond she shows up."

"Okay," I agreed. He hurried away.

Ethan sat next to me. He looked at my bare feet. "You should probably wash before putting on your socks. You could get some kind of infection."

"I'll be fine," I said. "My feet have stepped in worse stuff." I was referring to our neighbor's dog and the lovely packages he always left on our lawn. Ethan and I sat in silence for a little while, staring at the fountain. "What if . . ."

"No way." He folded his arms. "It's not possible!"

"But—"

"The Realm of the Gods cannot exist, Jax. It just can't."

"Why can't it exist?"

"Because that would mean . . ." He started chewing on his lip. "That would mean that Tyler's Cyclopsville game is based on *reality*."

"Hey, I didn't think of that." I looked back at the fountain. "How long has it been?"

"Two hours," he said, looking at his phone. "It's nearly eight o'clock."

"We'd better call home."

Ethan checked in with his parents, then I used his phone to call my mom. I didn't have to lie about the comic-book festival because I'd actually gone, so I told her about the costumes and the weird people. She wondered how Ethan had braved the crowds and I said there'd been a bit of anxiety but he'd quickly gotten over it. But the biggest lie was when I told her we had a place to stay for the night. After the calls, Ethan started searching again for a hotel room.

Tyler came back with sandwiches, sodas, and

a triple-shot espresso. While eating a turkey with Swiss, I watched the fountain. I only realized it had started to get dark when the park lights turned on. Ethan was real worried and kept talking about where we were going to sleep. I suggested that two of us could keep watch at the fountain while the other took a nap in the car. We'd rotate throughout the night. But the truth was, none of us wanted to miss the moment when she returned.

"*If* she returns," Ethan said.

Tyler called his friend Walker and discussed some Cyclopsville designs. Ethan read his Guinness book. I tried not to look away from the fountain but the photos in his book were really weird. One man had fingernails curled like snakes. Another man had hair growing on every inch of his face. But nothing could compare to what *I'd* seen—a girl who'd disappeared for real.

My eyelids started to feel heavy. I leaned against Ethan. And the next thing I knew, he was tapping my shoulder. "Huh?" I opened my eyes.

There she was, standing in the water, in the exact place where we'd last seen her.

17
ETHAN

FACT: *A wormhole and a portal are two totally different things. A wormhole is a shortcut through space-time, like a tunnel or a bridge, with each end residing in a different place. A portal is a gate or doorway that opens into a particular place. I know that fact because it was drilled into my head by my brother, one night last year, when our family was playing a board-game version of Jeopardy.*

Unlike Jax, my eyes had been wide open when the girl reappeared. But I had no idea if she'd used a wormhole, portal, or some kind of transportation device like they use in *Star Trek*. I did know, however, that those things were based on scientific principles, so they were a bit easier to accept than the magical urns.

"She looks different," Jax whispered.

She did. Her red hair was unbraided, hanging in crumpled waves. She wore a short dress that had a woven pattern along the collar and hem. But she had the same sandals that wound up to her knees. With her bag slung over her shoulder, she waded across the fountain. Tyler rushed over and helped her climb out. "I am pleased you are still here," she told him with a smile. "I brought you a gift."

As she opened her bag, my mood instantly changed from amazement to fear, as if a cobra might pop out. Or a deadly urn.

But she didn't pull out the urn. She pulled out a small glass vial filled with green liquid. She offered it to Tyler. "Drink."

"Uh . . ." I held up a hand. "I wouldn't drink that stuff if I were you." My brother had a tendency to shove anything that looked edible into his mouth.

I can't think of a single thing we drink that is naturally green, except for the wheatgrass juice my mom makes. Green is the color most often used in movies to represent things that are poisonous and/

or radioactive. Mouthwash is green, and so is engine coolant. If you drink the first you'll get sick, if you drink the second you'll die.

"Why's it bubbling?" Jax asked.

Like one of my father's lab experiments, the liquid frothed inside the glass vial, strengthening my belief that it was deadly. The girl put a hand over her heart as if we'd stabbed her. "You do not trust me?"

"We . . . we don't know you," I stammered.

"Look, we're very confused," Jax said. "You steal the urn. You disappear, you reappear. We don't know what's going on. You have a lot of explaining to do before one of us drinks that green stuff. Like, where did you go? And how did you get there?"

"I traveled to my world and presented the urn of Hope to Zeus."

"Zeus?" Tyler looked like he might wet his pants. "*The* Zeus?"

"Is there another Zeus?"

"Zeus is . . . *alive*? Tyler started to breathe really fast. We'd need to find a paper bag if he hyperventilated.

But why was I worrying about Tyler? What about *my* reaction? I felt dizzy all of a sudden, like I'd just gotten off a roller coaster. I needed to sit down. I needed to go home and read something that made sense. The world's longest fingernails made sense. The world's largest baby made sense. Zeus being alive did not.

A grin spread across Tyler's face. "This is so cool," he said. "You went to see Zeus! The main man. The king of the gods!"

"Yes, through the Poseidon Portal."

"Poseidon is a . . . *portal*?" Tyler's voice cracked. I'd never seen him so happy. He was acting as if Christmas had come in the middle of July.

"Wait a minute." Jax folded her arms across her chest. "What's a portal?"

"A gate or doorway that opens into a particular place," Tyler and I both replied, at the same time.

The girl nodded. "It is a temporary means of travel. But I don't understand why your sculptors and painters always portray Poseidon with a beard." She turned toward the reclining statue. "Why would a god who spends most of his life in the sea possess facial hair? Or any hair, for that matter?"

"Poseidon is bald?" Tyler asked. "Wow. I have to tell Walker to make some changes to our game."

"How do we know the urn's with Zeus?" Jax asked. "I mean, maybe it's still in your bag."

The girl turned the leather bag upside down and

shook it. Nothing fell out. "The urn of Hope will remain under Zeus's protection. Once I have delivered all three urns, Zeus will throw them into Hephaestus's fire. Since they were forged together, they must be neutralized together."

"Hephaestus is the blacksmith to the gods," Tyler explained to us.

"I know," Jax said. "I've been reading that book, remember?"

The girl held out the vial of green liquid. I had forgotten all about it. "Now that I have answered some of your questions, will you please drink this? It will relieve your pain."

Pain? I hadn't noticed Tyler limping, or complaining about a headache.

"I don't know what you're talking about," he said with a shrug. "I don't have any . . . pain."

She moved very close to him. They were the same height so their eyes were at the exact same level. As she stared deeply, he didn't blink. "The urn has not completely left you. There is still sadness. I saw it when we first met and I see it now. "

"You're wrong," Jax said. "He's feeling fine. He told us. Right Tyler?"

She pressed the vial into his hand. "The gods have

sent you this elixir, to remove the urn's ill effects. You will not remember the pain you suffered. You will be free of the lingering darkness."

Tyler's eyes widened. "Give me that!" He grabbed the vial and pulled out the little cork.

"Wait!" Jax and I both cried.

But the green liquid disappeared in one gulp.

I immediately thought about those drug commercials that list all the side effects. The list might begin with common things like headaches, dizziness, or sleepiness. But then it gets worse, like difficulty breathing, internal bleeding, and sudden death. Uh, sudden death is not a side effect. You can't recover!

After swallowing, Tyler wiped his hand over his mouth and stared into space. Jax and I watched, neither of us saying a word. My finger was poised over the phone, ready to dial 911 at the first sign of trouble—Tyler's lips turning blue, his eyes bugging out, his head spinning around. The liquid had been bubbling. Surely it wouldn't go down without some sort of side effect.

The girl stepped back. "How do you feel?" she gently asked.

"Better," he said, after a deep, satisfied sigh. "Way better."

"Your eyes are clearing," she told him.

"What are you talking about?" Jax stood on tiptoe and looked into Tyler's eyes. "They look the same to me." I agreed.

Tyler sighed again. "It's gone. It's really gone." He smiled with amazement, as if he'd been cured of cancer. "There's no darkness. I feel great!"

"What do you mean, there's no darkness?" I asked.

Tyler hesitated a moment. "I didn't want Mom or Dad to know that I was still feeling cruddy, so I pretended I was fine. If they knew, they would have sent me back to the hospital."

"But now you feel good? What was in that?" I asked. I took the vial from Tyler's hand and sniffed it. There was no odor. "If I take it to Dad's lab, he'd be able to break it down to its elements."

"That would be a waste of time." The girl took the vial and tucked it into her bag. "Tyler is cured by the gods. That is all you need to know."

"Cured," Tyler repeated. He smiled. "I feel better than ever."

"Wow," Jax said. "That's amazing." Then she laughed. "Do the gods have something that will cure Tyler of his BO?"

"Very funny," Tyler said, his smile fading. He turned away and sniffed under his arm.

The girl slung her bag onto her other shoulder. "Time moves much more quickly in your world, so we must make haste."

"We?" Jax asked.

"We have the same goal—to neutralize the urns. And we each have something the other needs. You can help find the urns in this world, and I can get them back to my world."

"Your world?" Tyler said. "Hey, what's your name anyway?"

She bowed, then said, "My name is—"

"I know what it is," I interrupted. "I figured it out."

Jax and Tyler looked at me with surprise. The girl raised her eyebrows, waiting for me to reveal her name. I didn't want to say it, because the act of speaking her name would be admitting that she was alive. That she was real. That the gods were . . . *are* . . . real.

I took a long breath, then said, "Your name is Pyrrha."

18
JAX

We were on the move again, heading down a path toward Tyler's car. My brain was getting pretty close to overloading.

Pyrrha? Seriously? A girl from a story. A girl who'd been given three urns, by Zeus, to make her happy, and then had those urns stolen by her father. She was here, in Boston. She'd come from the Realm of the Gods. And she wanted to join forces with Tyler, Ethan, and me.

This would make a great movie, no doubt about it.

As Pyrrha walked, her wet sandals left prints on the path. The hem of her tunic was soaked, too.

My feet were still wet inside my sneakers and it was kinda uncomfortable, but I didn't care. I was walking next to a girl from another world!

"I don't mean to be rude, but can you do a trick or something, just to prove you are who you say you are?" Ethan asked.

"She rematerialized in the middle of a fountain," Tyler reminded him. "She brought me a magic elixir. That's proof enough."

"Not really," he said. "If we're going to work together, then I'd like something more. Something I can measure, or record."

I didn't blame him for doubting. He tried to logic everything, but sometimes you just had to go with the flow. I walked on one side of Pyrrha, Tyler on the other. Ethan was at our heels. She smelled like freshly peeled oranges and mint. I desperately wanted those sandals. They'd look good with my purple jacket. "Are you immortal, like the gods?"

"Immortal?" She laughed. "Only the gods are immortal. But if you measure my life by your calendar, I am much older than any of you."

"You don't look older," Tyler said.

"Thank you." She smiled at him.

I squeezed between them. "I think we'd all feel

better if you explained some things."

"Which things?" she asked.

"Well, basically all things," I said. "We need you to explain *everything*." I turned around and looked at Ethan. "Right?"

"Yes," he said. "Start with how you found us."

She pushed her hair behind her shoulders. Lamplight caught in the sparkles, making her hair look wet. "We believed that the urns were forever lost in your world, and therefore, that they would not be a danger to humanity. But your great-aunt dug one up and opened it. The moment the magic was released, its power was felt on Olympus and the gods knew an urn had been found. There was no doubt that the urn needed to be returned to our realm, but there was debate about who to send and how, exactly, to get the urn without causing more disruption. But then your great-aunt went into hiding."

"You couldn't find her because no more magic was being released," I guessed. "So no one could sense the urn's location."

"Exactly." She continued. "Years later, when you, Jax, opened the urn of Hope in the city called Washington, DC, the gods again felt its power.

I volunteered to retrieve it, since it rightfully belonged to me. So I transported to the location where the magic had been unleashed."

"The Thomas Jefferson Memorial?" Tyler asked.

"Yes. Unfortunately, the urn was gone by the time I arrived. I watched as you were taken away in a medical chariot. I have been watching you ever since. But when you did not lead me to the urn, I searched your houses. I did not sense the urn's presence in either house."

"That's because we didn't have it," I said.

"You were inside our house?" Tyler asked. He scratched the back of his neck, looking a bit uncomfortable. "Did you go into my room? It's not usually so messy. I wish you'd called first. I would have cleaned."

Pyrrha smiled at him. She didn't say anything mean about how his room looked or smelled. I realized that she'd been nice to all of us through this whole thing. Even while we were chasing her, and even while we were doubting her, she'd been . . . nice. I wished I could be more like that.

"When it became apparent that you no longer possessed the urn, I was afraid it was lost forever. So I begged the gods to allow me to break one of their rules."

"What rule?" Ethan asked.

"Those of us who live in the Realm of the Gods are not supposed to communicate with this world. But Zeus gave me special permission to speak to you. So I followed you to the merchant's shop known as Merlin's Comics. I needed to get information from you."

"Information?" Tyler frowned. It was official. She'd talked to him because she'd been trying to find out about the urn. She hadn't been into him after all. He suddenly looked like he needed another hit of magic elixir. "That's why you left so suddenly? Because you'd gotten the information?"

"Exactly. You told me where to find your great-aunt and I needed to secure transportation." She put her hand on Tyler's shoulder. "But I would have liked to spend more time with you. Your gaming strategies are very interesting."

Tyler didn't need the happy elixir after all. Just a few words from Pyrrha and he was beaming again.

Pyrrha's strides were long so I had to quicken my pace. "I still don't understand. You got to Sisters of Mercy before us, so how did you find Juniper? She was listed as Jane Doe."

"As I got close, I felt the urn's presence," she

explained. "It led me to your great-aunt's room."

"Of course!" I slapped my hand on my leg. "That's why I didn't feel it. By the time we arrived, you'd already taken it."

"I climbed in through the window and introduced myself to the woman lying in the bed. She gave me the urn of her own free will." Pyrrha looked around. "Where is your chariot?"

"Not much farther," Tyler said, pointing down the path. "This city is crowded. It was hard to find an empty spot. And that has nothing to do with my parking abilities."

My head was still jammed with questions, but Ethan got the next one. "Why did you help us get away from Ricardo?" he asked. "You had the urn. You could have left the convention center and made it back to the fountain safe and sound, but you risked helping us. Why?"

"You needed help," she said. "Besides, I realized that I needed your help, too. There is a saying in my world that four heads are better than one."

"We have the same saying," I told her. "Only it's two heads are better than one."

"In my world, there are many multiheaded creatures, so four makes more sense."

"Cool," Tyler said.

"You still haven't explained where we're going or what we're doing." I said.

"My goal is the same as yours—to find the other two urns and neutralize them. The man named Ricardo is clever at hiding and he currently possesses the urn of Faith. We must find the urn of Love before he does."

"Ricardo has Faith?" I said. "But that means—"

"Ricardo is the bank robber," Tyler said, completing my sentence, which totally annoyed me. "He used Faith to steal money, then he followed us to Boston because he wanted to get Hope. Next, he'll try to find Love."

"Exactly," Pyrrha said.

"Wait a minute." Ethan scurried in front of us, then turned around and walked backward as he asked the following, über important question. "Why can't the gods find these urns?"

Yes! Exactly! Why were we going through all this when the gods had infinite powers to do whatever they wanted? Why didn't Zeus transport through Poseidon's portal and deal with this himself?

"The gods used to live in the human world but

it was a disaster. While some of the gods protected the human race, others pitted humans against one another for sport. They meddled in daily lives, destroyed without reason, pursued whatever they wanted for their own gain. It brought about a civil war and the only way the gods could save them-selves from destruction was to move away. Since that time, they have been forbidden to enter or interfere in the human world."

"But they gave you a vial of bubbling green stuff for Tyler," Ethan pointed out. "That's inter-fering, isn't it?"

"I took the vial," she said. "They did not give it to me. When I saw the pain in your brother's eyes, I felt compelled to save him." She looked at him as if she were looking at a cute puppy. "How could I allow such beautiful eyes to be marred by sadness?"

"Beautiful?" Tyler returned her smile. "My eyes are like Satyr dung compared to your eyes."

Wait a minute? Were they flirting? Eeeew.

"It's getting dark," Ethan said. "We still have no place to spend the night. What are we going to tell Mom and Dad when they call?" Then he bumped into something. "Oh, cool, look at this." We all stopped walking.

Ethan was distracted by an historic marker of some sort, which made perfect sense because he loved that kind of stuff. The bronze plaque had a drawing of some men dressed in Revolutionary clothing. Ethan began to read aloud:

When in the Course of human events, it becomes necessary for one people to dissolve the political bands which have connected them with another, and to assume among the powers of the earth, the separate and equal station to which the Laws of Nature and of Nature's God entitle them, a decent respect to the opinions of mankind requires that they should declare the causes which impel them to the separation.

"I do not understand," Pyrrha said. "What are these words?

Ethan's brain went into factoid mode. "That's the opening paragraph to the Declaration of Independence. It's a document that describes the reasons why this country was founded." He pointed to the words. "'It becomes necessary to dissolve the political bands' means that we didn't want to be ruled by England anymore."

"Why?" she asked.

"Because we didn't like their laws," Tyler said. "Their king was a butthead."

She read the next section:

We hold these truths to be self-evident, that all men are created equal, that they are endowed by their Creator with certain unalienable Rights, that among these are Life, Liberty and the pursuit of Happiness.

"You have the right to be . . . happy?" she asked. Then she laughed. "And the right to life and liberty? This is unheard of in my world. The gods take lives as they wish, and grant whatever they feel like granting. You are lucky they no longer inhabit your world."

I remembered some of those stories I'd read in the mythology book, about how the gods got jealous and turned a beautiful woman into a hideous creature with snakes coming out of her head. And how they tricked a man into murdering his own father. I guess it was a good thing that they'd moved out of the neighborhood.

A few minutes later, we reached Tyler's car. "So, where are we going?" he asked.

Pyrrha set her bag inside, then she removed the brown belt that had been wrapped around her waist. It was the same belt she'd taken to the Puzzle Master. I'd forgotten about the belt!

"When I collected the urn of Hope from your great-aunt's room, I found this." We all leaned close as she straightened the leather. A line of symbols had been printed from one end to the other.

"That's Greek," Tyler said.

"Yes, but the letters are jumbled. They make no sense." She ran her finger across the ink. "I asked your great-aunt but she could not remember anything about the belt. Her mind was confused."

"I bet I know what that is," Tyler said, taking the belt in his hands. He didn't know that Pyrrha and the Puzzle Master had already discussed this. "It's called a cipher. You need to wind it around a cylinder of the correct size. That's called a key. Then you can read the actual message."

"Does this have something to do with the urns?" I asked.

"Yes," Pyrrha said. "I have a feeling that it does."

If I could respect anything, it was an instinctual *feeling*. "Do you think Juniper has the key?" I asked. "We could go back to Sisters of Mercy and look through her stuff."

Tyler pointed a finger in the air, as if a great idea was about to sprout from it. "What if we already have the key? Something that's small and cylindric."

"The urn!" Ethan cried. Then his shoulders slumped. "Oops, the urn is gone."

"No problem," Tyler said. "We just have to find something that's the same size and shape. Hmmmm." He held out his hand. "It was about this big, right? The size of a cup, narrower at the base and getting wider near the top." He stuck his head into his car and rummaged around, then came back out with a huge grin on his face. And a Starbucks coffee cup.

We all watched as he wound the belt around the cup. Then he held it out to Pyrrha. "I can read some Greek but you'd better do this."

While Tyler slowly turned the cup, Pyrrha read. We listened, holding our breaths as if she were about to spill a classified government secret.

"The . . . lock . . . smith . . . will . . . unlock . . . love . . . with . . . a . . . kiss."

The locksmith? I inhaled so quickly, I started to cough.

"Do you know the meaning of this phrase?" Pyrrha asked. Everyone turned to look at me.

"Yes," I said. "Well, I don't know the whole meaning but I know who the Locksmith is. I've never met him, but he's—"

"Don't say anything!" Ethan cried. Then he motioned frantically. "I need to talk to you two. In private!"

Tyler and I joined Ethan on the sidewalk. He turned his back to Pyrrha, who was winding the belt around her waist again. "I just want to remind you that we're supposed to be going home tomorrow, remember?"

"We'll tell the parental units that we want to stay at the festival longer," Tyler said.

"Yes," I agreed. "We have to help Pyrrha find the urn of Love, Ethan. She's the only one who can destroy these things. That's what Great-Aunt Juniper wants. That's been her goal ever since she found the urn of Hope. When they're gone, she won't have to hide anymore. She'll be able to live a normal life."

"Not to mention the rest of the world won't be in danger," Tyler said.

"So you guys believe all this?" Ethan asked.

"That she's Pyrrha, and that the urn of Hope is with Zeus, in the Realm of the Gods?"

"Yes," I said. "As crazy as it sounds, yes, yes, yes."

"Me too," Tyler said. "And when this is over, I'm going to give her part ownership in Cyclopsville. She can help us make it totally authentic. Do you think she can get me some footage of a real Cyclops? That would be awesome!"

I ignored Tyler and put both my hands on Ethan's shoulders. I could tell by the way he was chewing on his lip that he was freaking out. "It's going to be okay," I told him. "We had already accepted all this stuff. We knew the gods were real, we knew that the urns were powerful. This is just a little bit more information."

"It's *a lot* more," he said. "The gods *still* exist."

I laughed. "Yeah. Pretty cool, huh?" This was the kind of realization that people would write books and songs about. This was as surprising as learning that Santa Claus was real. Or having a spaceship land in your backyard. I felt all bouncy inside, so I hugged Ethan, real hard. I even hugged Tyler. "Let's do this."

Then we all got into the car. "What did you

decide during your council?" Pyrrha asked. "Will you help me with the riddle? Do you know who the Locksmith is?"

"Yes," I said. "He's my father."

19
TYLER

REPORT #572A, FILED BY: Tyler Hoche, Team Captain

MISSION: Quest of the Secret Cipher

TEAM MEMBERS: Jax Malone, 2nd in Command

Ethan Hoche, Technical Officer

Pyrrha, Beautiful Visitor from Another Realm

TIME: 10:30 P.M.

LOCATION: Boston, MA

It was obvious from the start that our chances were slim. Thanks to my quick thinking and selfless nature, my crew had survived the prior quest in Washington, DC, though I'd barely made it out alive. Now, one month later, we found ourselves under the surveillance of a master criminal. This new quest was going to prove more difficult and, possibly, more dangerous.

While I was skilled in intelligence gathering and clandestine maneuvers, my ragtag crew were total newbs. My second in command was a girl who talked too much and got distracted by anything purple or glittery. The technical officer was a shy, nerdy boy prone to bloody noses and excessive worrying. We were doomed.

But then a new crew member arrived. She kissed my cheek. She said she was from another dimension. She was smart, beautiful, and mythological. I'd have to be careful around her. Too much time in her gaze and my brain might turn to mush. I let her sit in the front seat of my chariot.

She was our best hope for survival.

She brought a cipher, and using our combined mental prowess, we unleashed its code.

The Locksmith will unlock love with a kiss.

It became clear to us that the Locksmith was somehow involved with the urns, but before we set out to find him, the following intel was uncovered:

Pyrrha is a mortal, not a god.

The myth about Pandora's box is true.

Pyrrha came to our world to retrieve the urns of Hope, Faith, and Love.

We informed Pyrrha that after Juniper took the urn home, and as she tried to figure out a way to destroy it, she established a friendship with a man named Isaac Romero, aka the Locksmith, who happened to be the biological father of my second in command. Unbeknownst to the rest of us, the second in command had been in contact with the Locksmith via email. She'd uncovered his location—a top secret federal prison where he was serving time for breaking and entering. The technical officer located the coordinates on his iPhone and set a course. Parental units were called and lied to, a necessary component for the quest's success. I informed Pyrrha that she looked like a Aegean goddess in her blue dress. Second in command was demoted to third in command for telling me to stop acting so embarrassing and stupid.

With the newbs in the backseat and Pyrrha by my side, we set off on our quest. I did not question the circumstances. Pyrrha and I had been brought together by forces unseen. Seemed that love was in the air, and we were its victims.

20
JAX

It was way past our bedtimes. Tyler kept himself awake by guzzling lattes and pounding doughnuts. His gaming marathons had trained him to stay awake through the night, so I wasn't worried that he'd fall asleep at the wheel.

But I was crazy worried that Ricardo would find us again.

Ethan checked to make sure the GPS thingy was turned off on his phone. I watched out the back window. It didn't look like anyone was following. But how could I be sure? The Camels had stuck a tracking device under Great-Aunt Juniper's skin. Ricardo could have stuck one on Tyler's car.

How would we know until it was too late?

The prison camp was located fifty-seven miles from the nearest town. We'd run out of cash, and we couldn't use the credit card because if we did, our parents would probably find out that we lied about spending the night in Boston. So rather than getting a room at the last hotel we passed, we drove to a rest stop and parked. Then we slept in the car. Pyrrha drifted off right away, her head on Tyler's shoulder. Ethan totally hogged the backseat by stretching out his legs. It didn't really matter. I was too nervous to sleep.

I was going to meet my dad.

When morning came, we tried to clean up in the rest-stop bathroom. Ethan had a fit because there was no soap in the men's room so I had to squirt extra on my hand and bring it to him. I wished I could take a shower so I'd look nicer. I pulled my hair into a ponytail and put on a clean T-shirt and a pair of shorts from my backpack. Pyrrha didn't seem to need anything. Her dress looked great, and her hair had stayed perfectly smooth, even after car sleeping.

Tyler also changed his shirt, and borrowed some toiletries from Ethan. It was so obvious that he was trying to look good for our guest. "Did you rub that stuff all over your body?" I asked, cringing from the deodorant cloud that clung to him.

"I think he smells nice," Pyrrah said, sniffing Tyler's shirt. "Sandalwood?"

"Hypoallergenic sandalwood," Ethan corrected as he put the deodorant into his backpack.

We were out in the country, surrounded by trees. As Tyler drove the last few miles to the prison, we ate some gas station snacks. I rolled down the window. The fresh air was a welcome relief from Tyler's deodorant offgassing. Pyrrha leaned her arm on the door and stuck her face into the wind. I used to love doing that when I was little. As her hair rippled, it sparkled with bits of sunshine. We passed a sign that read, *Brookville Federal Prison Camp, Next Exit.*

"Why is your father in prison?" Pyrrha asked, turning to look at me.

"Breaking and entering into someone's private home," I said. "I guess he was trying to steal something. I don't really know."

"Both of our fathers are thieves," she said sadly. "My father created this catastrophe. We may need your father to help us end it."

Suddenly I didn't feel as ashamed. I wasn't the only girl who had a less-than-perfect parent. There were worse things a person could do than to steal. Maybe my father was a nice man who'd taken the wrong path. My mom had fallen in love with him, so he had to have a good side. And Great-Aunt Juniper had trusted him. There had to be more to him than the label "convicted criminal."

Ethan looked up from his phone. "Take this exit."

No barbed-wire fence surrounded the prison, no towers or armed guards ready to shoot anyone who tried to escape. It looked like a boring old office building. Two other cars were parked in the visitors' lot. A woman sat in her driver's seat, putting on makeup. Another woman and child were just getting out of their car. "Anyone want the last doughnut?" Tyler asked, holding up the box. My stomach clenched. If I never saw another doughnut again it would be too soon. Pyrrha, however, had said they were better than ambrosia. She grabbed the last one and ate it in two bites. Tyler watched, his eyes wide with respect. Here was a girl who could probably keep up with him in an eating contest.

It's weird how quickly you can get used to

things. Like when I had my braces. They hurt the first day but a few days later I didn't even notice them. And there we were, acting as if knowing a girl from a myth was perfectly normal.

"You look nervous," Ethan whispered to me.

"Understatement of the year," I said. How do you introduce yourself to a parent? It's supposed to be the other way around. "What if he doesn't want to talk to me?"

Ethan grabbed his baseball cap. "He made you that secret box."

"Sure, he made me a box, but that doesn't mean he wants me to come for a visit."

"This doesn't look like a prison," Pyrrha said. "Why is no one screaming in agony? Why is no one pushing boulders?"

Tyler leaned against the car. "Are you saying that those stories about Zeus's punishments are true? Sisyphus has to push a boulder up a hill every day, then start over in the morning? And Prometheus is chained to a rock while his liver is eaten by a giant eagle?"

"Yes, all true."

"That's barbaric," Ethan said. "Why would Zeus do that?"

"Sisyphus was a king who deceived the gods," Tyler explained. "And Prometheus broke Zeus's law and gave man fire, which is a major reason why mankind advanced scientifically."

"Zeus does not forgive those who disobey him," Pyrrha said, a note of sadness in her voice. Was she thinking about her father? Was he being punished in some horrid way for stealing the urns?

More cars drove into the lot. "Let's do this," I said.

We walked up to the security booth. One of the guards was watching something on his computer. The other was looking about as bored as I looked when I sat in math class, counting the minutes until the bell rang. "Hi," I said.

He sighed. "You here for a visit?"

"Yes. I'm here to see the Locksmith." Then I cleared my throat. "I mean, I'm here to see Isaac Romero."

He looked at the four of us. "Inmates are allowed two visitors per day, no more."

Ethan stepped back. "Pyrrha should go with you. I can wait out here."

"I need to see your IDs," the guard said. I pulled out my wallet and handed over my Chatham

Middle School ID. It was the dorkiest picture ever. My eyes were half closed and I looked like I was pooping. The guard grinned. "Why didn't you get a retake?"

"I was sick on retake day," I informed him, a bit snippily.

He made a copy of my ID, then set it on the counter. Then he held out his hand and looked at Pyrrha. This should be interesting. What kind of identification would she have? A student ID from Zeus's Academy or Hades High School? Maybe a gym membership from the Hercules Athletic Club?

She looked at me and shook her head. Then she stepped back.

So I grabbed Ethan's arm. "Come on. Let's go." I was actually relieved. I'd much rather have him by my side, especially since I was feeling like I might hurl. I couldn't remember ever being this nervous about meeting someone. Ethan showed the guard his Chatham Middle School ID. He was wearing his baseball cap in the photo, just like in real life. The school photographer was a friend of the family, so he'd let Ethan wear the hat, even though it was against yearbook policy.

The guard made a copy of the ID. "After you

go through those doors, you'll have to check in again." He handed the cards back to us.

"Take the belt," Pyrrha said. "You can show it to the Locksmith."

She started to wrap it around my waist but the guard said, "You won't be able to wear that. They make you leave belts, shoes, and bags outside the visiting room." He brought out a handheld metal detector and ran it over me. Then over Ethan. It beeped. Ethan took off his watch, then fished through his pockets. "Oops," he said, pulling out his phone, his Swiss Army knife, and an extra key to his house. He handed them to Tyler.

"Do you remember the code?" Pyrrha asked me.

"'The Locksmith unlocks love with a kiss,'" I said. She nodded. I looked worriedly at Tyler. "Keep a lookout for Ricardo."

"Roger that."

Once inside, we passed through another metal detector, and had to remove everything else from our pockets and put it into a tray. Gum, my wallet, his wallet, which were identical because we'd bought them at the Chatham Saturday farmers, market. We also had to leave our coats, shoes, and Ethan's hat. Then we signed in at the reception desk and were given visitor badges.

Twenty minutes passed. Maybe my father was trying to make up his mind whether or not to see me. Had we come all this way for nothing? My hands got sweaty. And my stomach still hurt. I tried to look at a magazine, but couldn't focus. Had Mom hidden the truth from me because my father was a bad person? Should I be afraid of him? Would Mom ground me for the rest of my life if she found out I'd been here?

A guard appeared in the lobby. "Jax Malone and Ethan Hoche?" he called.

As we followed the guard down the hall, I felt like I was walking into an operating room, about to be cut open and examined. Would he like me? Did that matter? We were here to figure out if he knew anything about the urns. If he didn't like me, my life wouldn't change. He hadn't been a part of it anyway. I told myself I didn't care. He was just a man and I needed him to help solve a riddle. Nothing more.

"I don't think we should say anything about Pyrrha," I told Ethan. "It's too complicated and it sounds crazy."

"I agree," he said.

We were ushered into what looked like a huge living room. Couches, love seats, and small tables were set up in a jumbled way. There were no glass partitions. A man in jeans and a white shirt was sitting in a corner talking to the woman who'd been putting on makeup. Another man, also dressed in jeans and a white shirt, was talking to the second woman and her child. Two guards sat on chairs in opposite corners, watching our every move. "Isaac Romero's over there," our escort told us. He pointed, then left.

Even though I'd read about minimum-security prison camps, I still expected a man dressed in prison stripes, with chains around his wrists and ankles, because that's the way it always looked in movies. So when he rose from his chair, I didn't realize I was looking at my father.

"Hello, Jax."

21
ETHAN

FACT: *The most famous prison in this country is Alcatraz, in San Francisco. Set on an island and surrounded by freezing water, it used to be a maximum-security facility, where the toughest and most violent criminals were sent. While some managed to escape, most were caught, drowned, or never found. Today, there is no evidence that any of those who disappeared survived. Other famous prisons include the Tower of London, which held two wives of King Henry VIII; South Africa's Robben Island, which was once a leper colony but then became the prison that held Nelson Mandela; and French Guiana's Devil's*

Island, where if you tried to escape you faced
piranha-infested waters.

I wanted to ask Jax's father if anyone had escaped from this prison, which looked more like a hotel. But we never got to that particular topic.

"I'm Isaac Romero." He held out his hand. Jax wiped her palm on her jeans, then shook. Maybe it was odd for a father and daughter to shake hands, but I think it would have been weirder if they'd hugged. I never understand why people I don't know want to hug me.

I waited a few feet behind Jax, trying to give her some personal space. Her dad wore a pair of jeans and a white shirt, same as the other inmates. The shirt had a stamp on the right breast pocket, *Brookville Federal Prison Camp*. His hair was dark, with some gray at the temples, and pulled into a ponytail like Jax's. His mustache and beard were trimmed into a goatee. His eyes were dark brown, as was his skin. Jax definitely looked more like him than like her mother.

People always tell me that I look like my mom and Tyler looks like Dad. Tyler definitely takes after Dad, with his math and science skills. Mom calls them the absent-minded professors because when they get interested in something, they forget about everything else. But I'm the only one with the allergies and the worries. I don't know where those came from.

"I'm Ethan," I told him, reminding myself to look into his eyes.

"Right. You're Cathy's son. I saw you once, but you were a toddler."

As I shook his hand, I wondered if there were lots of germs in prisons. "It's nice to meet you. . . ." What should I call him? Uncle Isaac didn't seem right. Mr. Romero sounded formal.

"Call me Isaac," he said.

There was a strong accent, definitely Mexican. I'd never been to Mexico but I'd met plenty of people who'd been born there. Our gardener, Roberto, was super nice and he always brought his cocker spaniel to play in our pool. And the woman who managed Tyler's favorite coffee bar, Taza de Café, always made Tyler a *café con leche*.

Jax shuffled. She didn't say anything, which was weird because she rarely got nervous. She'd go right up to anyone and ask a question. She'd grab the front seat at the movies and not worry if people were looking at her. But she wasn't even smiling. She looked like she'd eaten something that had made her sick. Maybe we should stop buying doughnuts and get some fruit.

"How 'bout we sit down," Isaac said.

Without a word, Jax sank into the nearest chair. I sat next to her. Isaac took the chair across the table. He placed his hands on the tabletop. His fingernails were trim and clean. Hard labor wasn't a part of his prison-camp life. Then he wrung his hands, a sign of nervousness. "Did something happen? Is your mother okay?"

Jax still didn't say anything. She just stared at him. "Aunt Lindsay's fine," I said.

He exhaled. He must have thought we'd come with bad news. That made sense. All those years without seeing us and then we show up, unannounced. He sat back in his chair and unclenched his hands. "Does she know you're here?"

"No."

"Who brought you?"

"My brother drove us," I said. "Tyler."

He nodded. "Yes, I remember Tyler. He was a smart kid." Then he met Jax's gaze and his face seemed to relax. "You have her eyes. Lindsay has the most beautiful eyes. I've never forgotten them."

That felt awkward. Silence filled the space between us. Jax fiddled with the hem of her shirt. "Uh . . ." I tried to help her. What should I say? "Uh . . . so how are you doing? Is the food good?"

He didn't take his eyes off Jax. "You didn't come here to talk about the food, did you? There's only fifteen minutes for visiting. If you've come to ask me some questions, you'd better get started."

Jax looked around. More visitors had entered the room. The conversation level was getting louder. If one of the guards wanted to eavesdrop on us, he'd have to scoot closer. Jax straightened her shoulders, summoning her courage. "I didn't know anything about you until this summer. Mom never told me your name. She pretended you didn't exist. Then Great-Aunt Juniper told me about you."

"How is she?"

"She had a stroke," Jax said.

His brow furrowed. "I'm sorry to hear that. She's a good friend to me. Is she going to recover?"

"She's okay except that she's confused about things. She was in the Museum of Fine Arts when she had the stroke. Now she can't remember stuff," Jax said.

He sat up. "The museum? In Boston?"

"Yes." Jax looked around again. She lowered her voice. "Do you know why she was there?"

"I might." He rubbed his neck but didn't say anything else. Was he waiting to see what we knew? I checked the clock on the wall. We were running out of time. "You still haven't told me why you're here."

"We're here because Great-Aunt Juniper asked us to help her find three very important . . . things," Jax said. She was being careful not to give too much away. The urns were still a secret and we had no idea if we could trust this man.

"Things?" One of his eyebrows arched.

"Yes. Old things. We found one," Jax told him, "but now we're looking for the second."

I hated not having my hat, especially because one of the guards kept staring at me in a real intimidating way, as if he expected me to suddenly jump up and initiate a prison break. "She gave us a clue," I told Mr. Romero. "But it's a riddle and we're hoping you can help us solve it."

He sat very still, his gaze moving between Jax and me, as if measuring our story. "What is the riddle?" he asked.

Jax described the belt, then she said, "'The Locksmith unlocks love with a kiss.'"

Isaac Romero tapped his fingers on the table. He

knew something. His eyes had flashed.

"Please," Jax said. "This is very important. Juniper is sick and you are the only person who can help. She needs us. You said in your email that you wanted to talk to her but you didn't know where she was."

He cocked his head. "My . . . *email?*"

"Yeah," Jax said. "Your email to me. The day before yesterday."

He rubbed the back of his neck again, a confused expression on his face. I sat very straight. "Mr. Romero? You didn't send Jax an email?" He shook his head. I looked at Jax. I could tell, by the way her eyes were narrowing, that she was coming to the same conclusion as me.

"Ricardo," she whispered. Then she smacked her hand on the table. "He tricked me. That's how he found us. He sent me fake emails, asking how I was doing, and telling me he wanted to talk to Juniper. I told him that I was leaving to see her. So he followed us. I can't believe I fell for that trick." Her cheeks turned red. "But I thought he was . . ." She hung her head. "I feel so stupid."

"You're not stupid, Jax." Isaac Romero reached out his hand, as if to pat hers, but hesitated. "Ricardo is a very clever man."

"You know him?" I asked.

"He is the reason I am in prison."

"What?" Jax and I both said.

"He double-crossed me. He double-crossed Juniper, too. He wanted the urn of Hope and the urn of Love for himself."

"You know about the urns?" Jax asked. "Then you *can* help us. We found Hope. Now we need to find Love."

Mr. Romero shook his head. "This is much too dangerous. You must go home and forget about this."

Jax fidgeted. "But we're already involved. Juniper chose us to help."

"You are children. You do not know what you face."

Jax scowled and squared her shoulders. "We know exactly what we face. We've been followed and chased and threatened with guns. We watched an urn suck Hope from Tyler's soul. We're not giving up, not now. We'll find the urn of Love with or without you." She sounded like her old self, no longer nervous and shy with this stranger. "Besides, you haven't been around so you can't tell me what to do." She folded her arms and glared at him.

Isaac Romero tapped his fingers on the table, his eyes narrow as he stared at his daughter. Then he stopped tapping and smiled. "I see you are my daughter after all. I will tell you what I know."

We leaned in close. Luckily, a woman and her husband were arguing about money, so the guards were distracted. Isaac Romero cleared his throat. "Juniper was in the Museum of Fine Arts because that is where she hid the urn of Love. She must have written the code on the belt so she would never forget it."

"But what does the code do?" I asked.

"I was hired to create the security system for the museum. Whenever I design a system, I include a back door, a secret way to disarm it. I gave this code to your aunt so she could retrieve the object when needed."

"So it's true," Jax said. "She was trying to break in."

"Not really. The object is hers. The museum is simply a hiding place. So even though she would disarm the security system, there would be no theft, technically." He lowered his voice. "The computer system is located on the first floor in a hidden room. The closest public room is the women's first-floor bathroom. To disable the system, Juniper would enter the women's bathroom, stand in one of the toilet stalls, and hold a smart phone close to the wall. This would give her the best chance to pick up the system's Wi-Fi signal. When the system asked her to log in, she would type the code."

"'Unlock love with a kiss,'" Jax said.

"There would be a slight flicker of the lights, nothing else. The system would appear to be working normally, but that would be an illusion. She would then have exactly fifteen minutes to remove her object. The system would restore automatically."

"So once it was disabled, she could get the urn and no alarms would sound?" I asked.

"Exactly."

I glanced at the guard. We now knew how to break into a museum. This was dangerous information.

"Where is the urn of Love hidden?" Jax asked.

"About fifteen years ago, your great-aunt donated two ancient busts to the museum. One is the head of Zeus, the other of Aphrodite. Aphrodite was damaged and had to be pieced back together. As Juniper worked on the restoration, she realized that the hollow space inside Aphrodite's head would be a perfect place to hide the little clay jar."

I glanced at the clock. Only another minute to go.

"If she has suffered memory loss from the stroke,

it is most important that you remind her to wait until just before closing. The staff will be tired and eager to leave. They are mostly college students and volunteers. They don't carry weapons but they can have police on the scene in under a minute."

Jax wiggled in her chair. "I'm wondering . . ." She closed her mouth and pursed her lips, as if holding back the question.

"You want to know why I didn't steal the urn for myself?"

"Yes," she said.

He smiled. "Because I'm not that kind of thief. I don't steal from good people."

The guard who'd escorted us to the visiting room returned and said, "Jax Malone and Ethan Hoche, your time is up. Please come with me."

I could tell by the way Jax was fidgeting that she wanted to ask many more questions. We stood. Mr. Romero shook my hand. "Nice to see you," he said. Then he shook Jax's hand, but as he did, he slipped her a small piece of paper. Then he pulled her close and whispered, "I know what you're planning. Please be careful."

22
JAX

I'd heard the saying, the apple doesn't fall far from the tree. Aunt Cathy always used it when she compared Tyler with his dad. Tyler had a wall of trophies, Uncle Phil had a wall of framed awards. Tyler got obsessed with his games, Uncle Phil got obsessed with his experiments.

Was I like my father? Could I deny it? I was preparing to disable a museum's security system and take a priceless object. Even if Great-Aunt Juniper hadn't gotten me involved with these urns, would I have been destined to this kind of life? I was always dreaming about traveling, about having adventures. And I'd tried to steal that candy bar.

I know what you're planning. Please be careful.

Had my father sensed I was like him? He'd squeezed my hand gently, as if he actually cared about me.

"What did he give you?" Ethan whispered.

I'd already tucked it into my pocket, but not before reading it. "His email address."

We collected all our belongings. Tyler and Pyrrha were waiting outside the security gate. Tyler was pacing, as if he needed to go to the bathroom. Pyrrha motioned for us to hurry. My purple coat swung from my hand as Ethan and I hurried down the walkway. "Better luck next year with your school photo," the guard called.

"What happened?" Pyrrha asked. "Did you solve the riddle?"

"Yes," I happily announced. "The urn of Love is hidden in the Museum of Fine Arts. The code disables the security system so the urn can be taken without setting off the alarms." Tyler kept pacing. "What's going on?"

"Ricardo robbed another bank," he said. "But this time, someone got killed."

We stood next to the car, in the shade of a large elm tree, and watched Tyler's phone. The CNN reporter, a man with a huge chin, pressed his earpiece as he spoke. An ambulance siren faded into the distance. "The robbery occurred at seven thirty this morning, at the Excelsior Bank in Boston."

The good news was that Ricardo had remained in Boston, so that meant he hadn't followed us. Phew! But that was the only good news.

"No official statement has been made by police or by Excelsior, but from eyewitness accounts, it appears that the robber approached the bank's manager in the parking garage that you see behind me. The manager had arrived a half hour before opening, as he usually did. People sitting in a café across the street thought they heard a storm and when they looked out the window, they saw garbage cans and garbage blowing out the parking garage's entry. Then the wind stopped and the bank manager and the alleged robber came out of the garage. The robber was carrying a bag, but didn't appear to be holding a gun. The bank manager walked in an odd way, witnesses said, as if in some sort of daze. Then they went into the bank."

He pressed his earpiece again. "We have a spokesperson here from the mayor's office." The camera shot widened as a woman stepped up next to the reporter. "Deputy Mayor Olson, can you tell us how the parking attendant died?" He held a microphone in front of her chin.

The deputy mayor spoke into the microphone. "He was an elderly man and it appears he had a heart attack."

"Do you think this is the same person who robbed the Excelsior Bank in Manhattan?" the reporter asked.

"Until the police make an official statement, we can't say for sure, but the similarities certainly point to the same man, or to two men working together. The weapon used seems to release a force like a gale wind that shatters glass and security cameras. In both robberies, the safe was emptied of cash. But here's what I find most interesting— in both events, the bank employees were easily manipulated and put into some sort of trance."

"Can you elaborate? What do you mean by a trance?"

The deputy mayor adjusted her sunglasses. "There were ten victims during the first robbery— seven employees and three customers. All remain under medical observation while officials try to determine what happened. Each victim remembers the same thing, that they felt scared when the robber first appeared. He opened some sort of container and a wind whipped through the bank. But after the wind settled, they no longer felt fear. They believed they knew him and that he had come to protect them. In fact, they all spoke of the robber in god-like terms, calling him all-powerful. They knew they needed to follow him, to do whatever he wanted. No one called police. No one tried to escape. They willingly opened the safe and helped him pack the money into bags."

"It sounds like some kind of hypnosis," the reporter said. "How is that possible?"

Tyler paused the news feed. "It sounds like the urn of Faith works differently from the urn of Hope," he said. "When hope is sucked from your soul, it leaves you feeling nothing, like an empty sack. But when the urn of Faith is opened . . ." He paused, his eyes narrowing as he put the facts together. "It sucks faith from your soul, which makes you desperate to believe anything—even that a bank robber is your savior."

We stood in silence for a moment. "Does that make Faith more powerful than Hope?" I wondered. "But why?"

"Faith is the act of believing in something," Ethan said. "I have faith in science. Some people have faith in religion. Others have faith that their government will take care of them. Or that luck will come their way. That things will work out."

I began to understand. "So if you're suddenly stripped of all your beliefs and you don't believe in anything, then you will be desperate to believe in something."

"Or in *someone*," Tyler said.

Pyrrha's eyes filled with tears. "I'm so sorry," she said. "Those urns were supposed to make me happy but they are hurting people. This is my fault."

"It's not your fault," Tyler said, wrapping an arm around her shoulder. "Ricardo is the one to blame. You did nothing wrong."

A sinking feeling hit me hard and I grabbed Ethan's arm. "Imagine what the urn of Love will do. If all the love is sucked out of you . . ." We all looked at each other.

"A person without love would have no empathy," Ethan said. "A person without love wouldn't care if others got hurt."

"There's no time to waste," Tyler said. "The Quest to Find the Urn of Love has begun. Museum of Fine Arts, here we come."

23
ETHAN

FACT: *Stealing an artifact from a museum is considered a felony. A felony is a crime that carries a one-year-or-more prison term. A misdemeanor is a crime that carries less than a year's imprisonment and/or a fine. Felonies include murder, assault, arson, and burglary. The length of time a thief is sent to prison is often determined by the value of the stolen object. We were about to steal a magical object. You can't get any more valuable than that.*

Jax kept saying we wouldn't be stealing, since the museum never purchased the urn of Love and had no idea that it was hidden inside Aphrodite's head.

"It's like getting something from the lost and found," she said. "Great-Aunt Juniper left it there and we're going to find it."

Well, I'm not sure Jax's logic was sound. We would certainly be vandalizing, and that's bad enough.

"Don't worry," Jax told me as we drove away from Brookville. "No judge or jury is going to throw us into prison. We're minors."

I didn't tell her that in some cases, minors could be tried as adults. We had enough to worry about. So instead of imagining what it would be like to spend the rest of my life in prison, I focused on the good news. Our parents thought we were spending a second day at the comic-book festival, so in a small way, returning to Boston made me feel better.

Jax told Pyrrha and Tyler everything that we'd learned from Isaac Romero. When she forgot the small details, I filled in.

Pyrrha stared out the windshield, not saying a word. Tyler kept glancing at her. "You okay?"

She didn't answer. Her shoulders were slumped. Was she thinking about the garage attendant who'd died? Was she feeling afraid, like me?

"We'd better make a plan," Jax said.

"Yes," I agreed. A plan was good. A series of directions leading to a determined outcome was better than winging it. A plan was something to focus on.

Here's what we decided to do. We'd locate Aphrodite's head. Then fifteen minutes before closing, Jax would enter the women's bathroom and type in the code using my phone. Once she'd disabled the system, she'd call Tyler. Then Tyler and I would create a distraction by getting into a loud argument. Because Pyrrha was the only one of us who wasn't terrified to hold the urn, she would open Aphrodite's head, get the urn of Love, then set the head back in place. Then we'd all meet in the lobby and walk out as if nothing happened. It sounded good. But as we all know . . .

. . . plans don't always go as . . . planned.

Pyrrha didn't say a word throughout the discussion. She'd been so nice and cheerful during most of this, I wondered why she'd suddenly become so quiet.

I found the museum's website. "It's one of the largest collections in the country, containing more than four hundred fifty thousand works of art. The head of Aphrodite is called the Bartlett Aphrodite. It's in the Greek and Roman Sculpture Gallery. That's number two-eleven on the map."

"Wait a minute. Today is Sunday," Jax said. "Is the museum open?"

"Yes, until four thirty."

"We'll have to use the credit card to get in," Tyler said. "But that's okay. Mom and Dad will love that we went to an art museum."

Pyrrha continued to sit in silence.

"What's the matter?" Jax asked. "Why are you so quiet?"

"I am afraid to fail," she said. "I am afraid to disappoint Zeus."

I shuddered. What would Zeus do if she didn't bring back the other two urns? I thought about Sisyphus and the boulder and Prometheus and the liver-eating. The worst punishment my parents had inflicted upon me was to make me give up watching the news. But that had only lasted two days.

Tyler put his hand on her shoulder. "You won't disappoint him," he said.

"But one man has died." Her eyes filled with tears. "What if more die? It will be my fault."

"It won't be your fault," Tyler said gently. "Your dad is the one who stole the urns and buried them. He's the cause of all this."

Pyrrha pulled away. "But I am my father's

daughter. In my world, if you share the blood, you share the blame."

"That's the stupidest thing I've ever heard," Jax said. "It's not our fault our fathers committed crimes. We are separate people. They make their own choices, we make ours. Besides, Ricardo is the one who's using the urns for evil. He's to blame."

Tyler scooted closer to Pyrrha and wiped a tear from her cheek. "Listen, if Zeus gives you a hard time, I'll talk to him."

My mouth fell open as I imagined that scenario. Tyler Hoche, telling the king of the gods to give his girlfriend a break? That was the most ridiculous thing I'd ever heard. Pyrrha must have thought so too, because she laughed. Then she said, "You have the heart of a hero."

"But the body of a gamer," Jax whispered in my ear. She stuck a finger in her mouth and pretended to gag. I agreed. It was bad enough that we were in this predicament, but having to watch Tyler and Pyrrha flirt was making it worse!

It was late afternoon when we reached the museum. The sidewalk was crowded with tourist groups. There was even a group of comic-book-festival people, dressed like ninja pirates. After Tyler found a parking spot, I downloaded an image of our target. "Here she is," I said, showing them the photograph. Aphrodite's head was carved in stone and mounted on a stand. A portion of her nose was missing, as if she'd been dropped on her face. Tyler began to open the car door when I said, "Can we please go over the plan again?" I'd started to feel uneasy and I wanted to make sure I'd memorized all the details.

That's when my phone rang, which reminded me that we needed to check in with our parents. But then I read the screen.

Incoming call from Ricardo.

Jax scooted across the seat. "Can he trace us?" she asked.

"He shouldn't be able to. The GPS is still disabled."

She yanked the phone from my hand before I could stop her and pressed *Accept*. "This is Jax Malone."

Tyler and Pyrrha turned around, watching from the front seat. Jax pressed the speaker button and a familiar voice filled the car. "Hello, Jacqueline. How are Ethan and Tyler? I hope you are all well."

My body immediately went into fight-or-flight mode. As adrenaline flooded my veins, my heart began to pound, my hands began to sweat, and my stomach tightened. I wanted to go home and hide in my room. I wanted Ricardo to go away!

Jax scowled at the phone and tightened her grip, her fingertips turning white. "Don't pretend you care about us. What do you want?"

"Give me the urn of Hope and I will reward you. How does one hundred thousand dollars sound?"

"We don't want your stolen money. A man died because of you!"

There was an exasperated sigh. "People die every day. Those who stand in my way will suffer the consequences. But there is no need for you, Ethan, or Tyler to suffer. You can join me."

"Join you?"

"The Camels were imbeciles, Jacqueline. I should never have hired them. But you are smart. With Hope, Love, and Faith in our hands, we can rule the world."

She put her hand over the speaker and whispered to us, "He wants to rule the world? He's totally crazy."

"This is just like a comic book," Tyler whispered back.

"Ask him why he robbed those banks," Ethan whispered.

She uncovered the speaker. "Why did you rob those banks?"

"Every great venture needs funding, Jax. And

with enough money, I can have anything I want. And so can you, but only if you join me."

Jax took a deep breath, her eyes flashing. "We'll never join you!"

Ricardo chuckled. "You do not understand, do you Jax? The urns are too powerful for children to manage. But I know how to wield them. I understand their potential." He paused. There was a clicking sound, then came the question that sent a chill straight up my spine. "Why are you at the Museum of Fine Arts?"

Jax gasped. We looked out the windows. Was he watching us? Was he parked outside? How would we recognize him?

Pyrrha pointed at the phone. "Leave them be!" she said.

"Who is that?" Ricardo hissed. "Who is with you?"

Pyrrha put a hand to her mouth, realizing that she shouldn't have spoken. The last thing we needed was to reveal her identity to Ricardo. He'd paid people to kidnap Great-Aunt Juniper. I imagined he'd do anything to get his hands on the one person who knew more about the urns than any other person in this world.

Tyler grabbed the phone from Jax. Then he used the same obnoxious voice that he used for his voice-mail message. "Hello, Ricardo. This is Tyler Hoche. I'm going to propose an entirely different scenario. You give us the urn of Faith and we won't contact the police and give them your phone number."

"I thought you were a genius, Tyler Hoche. You know, as well as I, that we cannot involve the police in this matter. Can you imagine what would happen if the government got its hands on one of the urns?" As he paused, we heard the sound of an engine starting. "Boston is a lovely city. Are you going to the museum for a particular reason?"

"We don't know what you're talking about," Jax said, a slight tremor to her voice.

"I know you are outside the museum at this very moment. I will meet you there shortly and we can discuss—"

Jax ended the call. She stared at me, wide-eyed. "What do we do?"

"He's still tracking us," I realized. "It wasn't my phone after all. He's put a tracking device somewhere else. I bet it's on the car."

"We do not have much time. He said he would meet us shortly." Pyrrha grabbed the door handle. "That means he is not here yet. But he is on the way."

I swallowed hard. Rule the world. That's what

he'd said. Was that every villain's goal? "What if he turns the urn of Faith on us?" I asked. "He could convince us to tell him everything we know. He could convince us to help him." That was a horrid possibility. I shuddered. "I have my allergy shots on Wednesday. Is it too late to turn back and forget any of this happened?"

"We can't let him trap us," Jax said. "But we'll have to deal with him eventually because he has Faith. The urns can't be destroyed until all three are delivered to Zeus. Isn't that what you said?"

"Yes," Pyrrha confirmed.

There were too many challenges to face. I didn't know where to begin. "What do we do?" I asked, my voice cracking.

"The best way to get through Cyclopsville and to the Cyclops king is to do one thing at a time," Tyler said calmly. "The strategy is the same for us. We focus on the task at hand—getting the urn of Love. Then we'll deal with the urn of Faith."

"You do not have to risk your lives," Pyrrha told us. "Your monument stated that you have the right to life, liberty, and the pursuit of happiness. You are not obliged to help me. I will understand if you wish to end this quest."

We looked at each other. For a moment I wanted to yell, *Yes! End the quest!* But I didn't. Because I knew that no matter how terrifying this was, we had to do it. We had to succeed. Because no one else could do it for us.

And if Pyrrha failed, then she'd have to face one of Zeus's punishments.

"Let's go," I said.

Jax grabbed her purple coat. I made sure my baseball cap was secure. And we scrambled out of the car.

As we walked toward the museum, we passed by a huge statue of a Native-American man sitting on a horse. He was bare-chested and wore a loincloth and a headdress. His arms were spread wide and his face was turned up to the sky. The statue's plaque read, *Appeal to the Great Spirit*. "He's asking his gods for help," Pyrrha said. "I only hope his gods are more forgiving than mine."

So did we all.

24
JAX

The guard at the museum's entrance was checking people's backpacks and purses. Because the urn of Love was so tiny, Pyrrha had decided to leave her leather bag in the car. We didn't want to be slowed down by security checkpoints.

Tyler paid our entrance fee. The cashier warned us that the museum was closing at four thirty so we didn't have much time. Ethan grabbed a map off the counter. But it turned out he didn't need it.

"Look," I whispered. Pyrrha was walking up a grand staircase, as if she knew exactly where to go. "She can feel the urn," I realized. "Go follow her. I'll head into the bathroom. We have to be quick."

Ethan handed me his phone. It was four

o'clock. "Isaac said that the system will be disabled for fifteen minutes. If you do it at exactly four fifteen, that'll time perfectly with the museum's closing. Do you remember what to do?"

"Yes." Then I whispered, "'Unlock love with a kiss.'"

"Where should we meet?" Tyler asked.

"Back at the car," I said. "Hurry. Pyrrha's already upstairs."

Ethan and Tyler took off. There was no time to worry. No time to question our plan. "Where's the ladies' bathroom?" I asked the woman at the ticket desk. She pointed the way. As I walked, I repeated the plan over and over in my head. Go into the bathroom, stand close to the back wall, find the Wi-Fi signal, type in the code. *You can do this*, I told myself. *Unlock love with a kiss.* As I got closer to the door, my legs began to feel wobbly. I glanced over my shoulder. No Ricardo. No guards. No one suspecting that the girl heading for the bathroom was going to mess around with the security system. I pushed the door and stepped inside.

"Oops. Sorry," I said as the door bumped into a woman.

Crud! There was a huge line for the toilets!

Why is there always a line? This is never a

problem in the men's room. At least, that's what Ethan's told me. Do men pee faster? Maybe that should be my next science fair experiment. I squeezed inside. Why had everyone waited until just before closing time? Yeesh!

One stall opened. A lady came out, another lady went in. The line moved an inch. Another stall opened and the line moved another inch.

It was 4:06. *Come on, people*, I wanted to holler. *Hurry up and pee!*

At 4:07, my heart began to pound. Why was everyone taking so long? Something had to be done.

Two old ladies stood at the front of the line. They were dressed in nice suits and heels and were talking about where they were going to have dinner. One of them wanted seafood but the other wanted to try a new Thai restaurant. They started to argue. A pregnant lady stood third in line. Would it be totally rude if I asked to cut?

Why was I worrying about being rude? The fate of the world was at stake!

I thought about Ethan, Tyler, and Pyrrha. Had they found Aphrodite's head? Were they paying attention to the time? I hoped Tyler wasn't getting distracted by all the ancient art, and that Ethan wasn't trying to memorize the map, or factoids, instead of creating a distraction.

At 4:10, I started bouncing on my heels. Another stall opened. The first old lady took a step. "Excuse me," I called in my sweetest voice, the one I saved for Mom when I needed to convince her of something—like letting me go to a comic-book festival. "May I please cut ahead of you?" I wiggled. "I really, *really* can't hold it."

"Oh dear," she said with a worried look. "I know exactly how that feels. Go ahead, sweetie." She stepped aside.

"Thanks." Yes! Success!

I slipped into the stall, then closed and bolted the door. The toilet next to me flushed. Water ran in the sinks. I checked the phone: 4:12. Almost time. I held it up to the wall, searching for the Wi-Fi signal. Where was it? Come on, come on.

An announcement blared from somewhere overhead. "The museum will be closing in fifteen minutes. Please make your way to the coat-check room to collect all your belongings. Once again, the museum will be closing in fifteen minutes. Thank you for visiting today and we hope to see you again soon."

My hands started to shake.

Where was the signal?

25
ETHAN

FACT: *Distraction is a great way to stay calm. I learned that from my counselor. We can control our thoughts by changing our focus. If something makes you nervous, think about something else.*

When my heart started pounding and I felt like running back to the car, I unfolded the museum map and focused on its intricate design. *Do not think about the fact that you are about to steal something,* I told myself. *Do not think about all the laws you are going to break. Instead, memorize this page of information.*

"This is the Huntington staircase," I said as Tyler and I followed Pyrrha. The museum didn't appear to be very crowded. Jax was already in the bathroom. She'd never been good with technical stuff, so it worried me a little that she was the one who was going to disable the security system. She got impatient when things didn't work the way they were supposed to. That's why she didn't currently own a phone. She'd gotten mad at it because the battery kept dying. So, in a fit of frustration, she threw it into the river.

If anything goes wrong, please don't throw my phone into the toilet.

"The artist is John Singer Sargent," I said as we passed beneath a huge domed ceiling that was covered in murals of Greek and Roman gods. Did any of these portraits resemble the real gods? I might have asked that question but Pyrrha kept walking, as if pulled by a leash. "This is the Upper Rotunda," I said, reading the map.

"What does Ricardo look like?" Tyler asked as he checked over his shoulder.

"Tall," I said. "Skinny. He was wearing black clothes and a fedora." I stumbled as I turned around. Lots of people were staring up at the murals. But there was no fedora in sight. At least, not yet.

We took a right turn, into another wing. We passed a couple of Egyptian statues, then a huge marble statue. "That's a king named Menkaura and his queen," I said. "And that's the goddess Juno."

Tyler whipped around. I expected him to say something mean and call me Factoid Boy. But instead, he whispered, "Good work. Keep pretending to be a tourist. The guards won't suspect a thing."

Guards?

I'd forgotten about them. My arms fell to my sides. Sure enough, guards stood in the corners of the gallery. The good news was, they didn't appear to carry guns. The bad news was—there were a lot of them. I stuck the map in front of my face again.

We took a left. "This is the Italian Renaissance Sculpture and Decorative Arts Gallery," I said.

"Is Pyrrha going in the right direction?" Tyler asked.

"Yep," I said. "Gallery two-eleven is up ahead."

We took a right and entered another room that was filled with Greek and Roman artifacts. Only one guard stood in the corner. Four people were passing through. Pyrrha had stopped walking and was standing in front of a pedestal. She hadn't needed the map to find Aphrodite's head. I glanced around, my heart pounding in my ears. No Ricardo. The security guard wasn't paying any attention to us. She looked bored. I looked at the wall clock: 4:06. Nine more minutes and the lights would flicker. I sneezed. Oh please nose, don't start tingling!

"It's gone," Pyrrha said.

"Huh?"

A little sign mounted on the pedestal read, *Bartlett Head*. This was the right place. But the glass case on top of the pedestal was empty. A temporary sign had been taped below. *Removed for cleaning*.

"Oh no," I said with a groan.

"We've reached the first obstacle," Tyler said as he folded his arms and stared at the empty case. "In a quest story, obstacles almost always come in groups of three. Every game designer knows that."

I didn't point out that we weren't playing a game.

"It was here, just a moment ago," Pyrrha said as she walked slowly around the pedestal. "The energy remains, as if it left a footprint. I can feel it."

Without Aphrodite's head, the plan was ruined. "What do we do?" I asked. "Should we call Jax and tell her it's over?" Maybe it was better this way. The urn seemed perfectly safe in Aphrodite's head. Pyrrha could return, by herself, and deal with it some other time. And we could go back to living our lives in Chatham. Tyler would spend the summer working on

Cyclopsville. Jax would scour garage sales for travel guides and I could go to the library, sit in the quiet room, and read whatever I wanted to read.

"It is not over," Pyrrha said. She was looking toward the end of the gallery. "The energy leads in that direction. It is not far. We have not failed." Her voice was determined, and she wasn't going to give up, which was something else she and Jax had in common.

"Don't panic," Tyler said. "Three heads are better than one. We can figure this out."

"I thought it was four heads," I corrected.

"You kids looking for the Bartlett Head?" We hadn't noticed the guard. She'd moseyed over and had been listening to our conversation.

"Yes," we all said.

She stood with her feet set wide apart and her arms folded. Her hair was pulled into a tight bun. "The curator just removed it, about ten minutes ago. Cute little thing." She cleared her throat. "Uh, the head, that is, not the curator. He's a bit homely, in my opinion."

"Where is it?" Tyler asked. "We need to see it."

"We need to see it *immediately*," Pyrrha said.

"Sorry to disappoint you, kids, but the Bartlett

Head is currently in the maintenance room."

Pyrrha looked toward the hallway. "Down there?"

"Yes, but I can't take you in there. It's against the rules. Besides, it's almost closing time." She checked her watch. "Yep, sixteen more minutes and I'm outta here."

Maybe the plan would still work. "Do you need a key to get into that room?" I asked. "Or is it wired into the security system?"

The guard raised an eyebrow and looked at me as if I were up to some kind of mischief. Which I was. Had that question been too obvious? Had I blown it? Was she going to call for backup? Or throw us out?

"We're writing a report for school," Tyler said. "About the museum. That's why we're asking so many questions." He smiled politely at her.

She relaxed her expression and nodded. "Kids are always coming here to write reports. If you ask me, they give out too much homework these days. The door is wired into the security system. An alarm will sound if I try to take you in there. Sorry. You'll have to apply to our educational department if you want to get a private behind-the-scenes tour."

An announcement filled the gallery. "The museum will be closing in fifteen minutes. Please make your way to the coat-check room to collect all your belongings. Once again, the museum will be closing in fifteen minutes. Thank you for visiting today and we hope to see you again soon."

Time was up. It didn't matter now if Jax was successful or not. The urn of Love was behind a locked door and there was no way we could—

Pyrrha groaned and grabbed her stomach. "I am not well," she said. "I feel dizzy." Then she stumbled forward. Tyler tried to catch her but was too late. She bumped against the guard and collapsed to the floor. Then she lay on her side, moaning.

I dropped the map. What was going on? Was this some sort of godly intervention? Had Zeus decided to punish her already?

"Pyrrha?" Tyler said, kneeling next to her. "What's wrong?"

She squeezed her hands into fists. "It hurts. The pain is unbearable!"

Tyler darted to his feet and pleaded with the guard. "Why are you just standing there! Call someone. Get some help!"

The guard looked just as shocked as the rest of us. One moment Pyrrha had seemed perfectly well, the next she was on the floor writhing. The guard pulled a walkie-talkie from her belt. "Joe, we have a medical emergency in gallery two-eleven. Hurry!"

Pyrrha curled into a ball, her face clenched in agony.

Though my mind was spinning, I stood frozen in place. We'd learned basic first aid in health class but that was in case someone had a heart attack or drowned. We'd never learned what to do if a Greek god imposed some kind of magical punishment.

The security guard rushed into the next gallery, calling for more help. I knelt beside Pyrrha. "What can I do?" I asked. Should I run downstairs and get Jax? Should I get her some water? A blanket?

She stopped moaning, looked at me, and winked.

She was . . . faking?

"Go get the urn," she said.

Tyler handed me his phone. "Go!"

Why had we even bothered to make a plan, if we were going to turn it completely upside down? I was supposed to be the distraction. She was supposed to get the urn. Then, as the guard returned with another guard, Pyrrha started moaning again.

I backed away as the two guards rushed to Pyrrha's side. Her groans turned to screams. She was a pretty good actress.

No one was looking at me. Tyler told the guards that his girlfriend might be having a seizure, then shot me a look that clearly said, *GO!*

I'd failed to create a distraction in time, so Pyrrha had taken over that role. Now it was up to me to steal the urn. Ethan Hoche. The kid who got nervous in crowds. The kid who needed allergy shots. The kid who always got nosebleeds in stressful situations.

Nose—don't fail me now!

I turned and ran from the gallery until I found the door. *Maintenance Room. Entry Prohibited. Alarm Will Sound.*

Tyler's phone read 4:16. Over in gallery 211, Pyrrha was still putting on her performance. No one was watching me. But I couldn't open the door until Jax disabled the system. My fingers twitched, waiting for the moment when the phone rang or the lights flickered.

Jax? What are you doing?

26
JAX

My hands were shaking. This was crazy. I was about to hack into a security system that had been designed by my own father. Mom would totally kill me if she ever found out!

Last summer, my biggest worry had been deciding whether or not to spend my hard-earned babysitting money on a new bike. Things sure change quickly.

I held the phone close to the wall, watching as it searched for a Wi-Fi signal. Then four bars appeared. *BMFASecurity.* "Woo-hoo!" I shouted.

"You okay in there?" a lady asked.

Oops. I'd forgotten that there were still people

in line for the toilets. "Yes," I said. "I'm fine. Just relieved." Yeesh. Why had I said that? Oh well. There were other things to worry about than having a bunch of strangers think I was pooping.

I tried to log in to the system, but it asked for the code. This was it. I began to type.

Unlock love with a ko . . .

Oops.

. . . with a ko . . .

My thumbs felt like they were made of dough. I was shaking so much, I couldn't control where they landed. So I closed my eyes and took a deep breath, reminding myself what was at stake. The urn of Love might have been the smallest of the urns but it seemed to me that of all the things that could get sucked from your soul, love would be the worst.

If I didn't love Ethan or Tyler, I wouldn't be worried about them getting caught. If I didn't love Great-Aunt Juniper, I wouldn't be trying to protect her. If I didn't love my mom, I wouldn't worry about upsetting or disappointing her. If I didn't love myself, I wouldn't care about anything. If no one cared, people like Ricardo could do whatever they wanted. And now there was someone new in my life—my father. I didn't know him very well but there was a chance that I'd come to care about him, too. Maybe even love him.

Unlock love with a kiss

I held my breath. Nothing happened. I read the code. It was spelled correctly. Why wasn't it working? Another toilet flushed. Had I done something wrong?

Then, the lights flickered.

27
ETHAN

FACT: *No time for facts.*

The lights blinked. The phone rang. "It's disabled," Jax's voice said. She was whispering. I heard a toilet flush. "You have fifteen minutes."

"Twelve," I pointed out.

Gripping the lever, and expecting a siren to blare, I opened the door. Then I slipped inside and shut the door behind me.

It was dark in there. I felt along the wall until my fingers rested on a switch. *Click.* Two fluorescent bulbs turned on and I found myself face-to-face with an Egyptian statue. I gasped.

"What happened?" Jax asked. "Are you okay?"

"No, I'm not okay," I said as I looked around the room. It was as cluttered as Jax's garage, but without the My Little Pony swimming pool. "I was supposed to be the distraction but the Bartlett head wasn't in the gallery so everything got messed up. Now Pyrrha's pretending to be dying of some stomach flu and I'm trying to find the Bartlett Head."

"What?"

"There's no time to explain."

"Okay. I'll wait for you on the front steps. I'll call if I see Ricardo. Good luck."

Luck was overrated. At least, that's what I'd always thought. I stuck the phone in my pocket and scanned the room. There were two tables cluttered with clay pots, jars, and tools. Crates and sawdust were scattered around the floor. Empty frames leaned against the wall. I nearly tripped on a marble vase. Just as I started to sweat, I saw it.

The small stone head sat on a counter, next to an empty Starbucks cup. Aphrodite's face stared at me. She looked bored, like she was tired of being in this museum. I wondered if she looked like this in real life.

My world was real life. But her world was real life

too. And if I wasn't successful, the two worlds would collide in a disastrous way.

I picked up the head and turned it upside down. Where was the urn? I felt along the bottom, looking for a release mechanism or a crack, anything that might open a secret compartment. I pressed my fingers over her face, her hair, the back of her head. Then I turned her over.

There it was. The bottom of the neck slid to the side. I reached with two fingers and pulled out a tiny clay pot. The urn of Hope had been painted black with white swirls. This urn was bright red—the color of fresh blood. Or the color of a valentine. As I touched the magical urn, I expected the strange voice to fill my head. But nothing odd happened. Then I remembered how Juniper had explained the sensation to us. She and Jax had both touched the urn of Hope and could hear its voice because they were female. The urns had been created for a girl, so it sought a girl's protection. But holding the urn had no effect on me. It simply felt like an ordinary clay pot.

As I stood, holding that tiny artifact, the moment felt suspended in time. My science brain whispered to me, Go on, open it. It's a clay urn. There's no way it can drain love from people. That's scientifically impossible. Everything you've seen up to this moment has been illusion or delusion. A scientist can find the rational explanation. There are *always* rational explanations.

But I now knew that the truth was bigger. For there are also mysteries. And magic. And luck.

So I closed Aphrodite's head, set it upright, and headed for the door.

With the urn hidden in my hand, I hurried into gallery 211. Five guards and a bunch of tourists were gathered around Pyrrha, who was moaning like she was possessed by demons. "She's having a seizure," someone said.

"Maybe she's got food poisoning," someone else guessed.

I waved at Tyler. He nodded, then grabbed Pyrrha's hand and pulled her to her feet. "I am cured!" she announced to the crowd. She pushed hair from her eyes and smoothed her dress. "Thank you for your assistance," she politely told the guards. Then she and Tyler pushed through the onlookers and followed me out of the gallery. I wanted to run, but that would look suspicious. But I walked as quickly as I could, the little urn clasped within my fingers.

"Hey!" our guard called. "The ambulance is on the way. You should see a doctor."

"We'll go see our family doctor," Tyler called. "Thanks again."

I was halfway down the staircase, Pyrrha at my heels. When I reached the ground floor, I looked back. Tyler was close behind. The security guard stood at the top of the staircase, her hands on her hips, a very concerned look on her face. "Keep moving," Pyrrha whispered to me, tugging on my arm. We joined the other patrons who were heading toward the exit. No alarms had gone off. We were almost there.

But wait. This had been too easy. Tyler said there were always three obstacles. I'd slipped into the maintenance room and slipped out, undetected. Was our quest complete, or would something else stand in our way?

Adrenaline coursed through my veins as I charged outside. This was undeniably the most stress I'd felt in a long time. I was holding a vial of magic in my left hand but the thing that amazed me the most was the fact that my nose wasn't bleeding. Not even a tingle. I could barely believe it. My body wasn't freaking out on me. It was a moment, like when I took my first step, or when I swam across the swimming pool for the first time.

Jax wasn't waiting for us on the steps, but that didn't worry me because the original plan had been to meet at the car. We broke into a run, Tyler in the lead. I kept my eyes peeled for any sign of Ricardo. But the coast looked clear.

We were all panting by the time we reached the car. "You got it?" Tyler asked. I opened my palm, revealing the little urn. Pyrrha was about to reach for it, when Tyler asked, "Where's Jax?"

I closed my fingers. Jax should have been here. She should have been waiting.

The last few tourists streamed out of the museum's entryway, but not a single girl with frizzy black hair and a purple jacket was among them. Tyler pulled out his phone. No answer. Then I pulled out mine and pressed her number. No answer.

A terrible sensation washed over me. I knew something was wrong. It was one of those unscientific moments that Jax was always talking about—it was a *feeling*. My legs got heavy. All the sounds around me—the thrum of traffic, the chatter of people— disappeared.

Was this the second obstacle?

Then the phone rang.

Tyler grabbed it and pressed the speaker button.

"Hello, Tyler. Hello, Ethan. Are you ready to turn over the urn of Hope?" There was no doubt who was speaking. Ricardo's voice was unmistakable and it made my blood turn cold.

"Don't give it to him!" It was Jax, but her voice was coming from the phone.

"Jax?" I cried. What was she doing with Ricardo?

"That is correct," Ricardo said. "Jacqueline is with me. And I will keep her unless you are willing to make a trade."

He was here, at the museum. He was here and he'd taken Jax!

Tyler, Pyrrha, and I whirled around, searching the parking lot, searching the street. Where was she? Then Pyrrha grabbed the phone. "Do not hurt her! Do you hear me, Father? Do not injure Jacqueline Malone!"

Tyler and I froze. *"Father?"* we both said.

"Pyrrha?" Ricardo's voice softened. "Is that you? What are you doing in this world? You are forbidden to be here. You are breaking Zeus's law."

Tyler and I looked equally shocked, our eyes wide, our mouths hanging open. Ricardo and Epimetheus were the same person? Ricardo was an alias? We watched and listened as the story unfolded before us.

"I came to save you, Father." Pyrrha's eyes filled with tears. "You promised Zeus that you would find the urns and destroy them. But you broke your promise. He will imprison you for eternity. I begged him to give you one last chance. That is why I am here. If we return the urns, and they are destroyed, once and for all, you will be forgiven. But if you do not return . . ." She cringed. "Please, Father, stop this madness. Zeus has Hope and—"

"You returned Hope?"

"Yes. And I will return Love and Faith. And then we can be a family again. Please, Father, come home with me. Mother misses you. The gods will forgive."

"The gods never forgive. They cannot be trusted. Why would I go back to a world where I have no power, when this world offers me wealth and glory beyond measure? Come to me, my darling daughter, and together, we will rule this world."

Tears streamed down Pyrrha's cheek. Her father was a monster and she was trying to save him. But the monster had Jax.

Tyler grabbed the phone. "Listen to me, you're wasting your time. You can't rule the world. It never works. It always ends the exact same way. Don't you read comic books?"

"Let Jax go!" I yelled into the speaker. "If you let her go, we'll give you the urn."

"Please, Father, don't hurt her. Jax is my friend."

"Give up your quest, Pyrrha, and she will not be hurt." Then the phone beeped. The call had ended.

Tyler pressed *Redial* over and over, but the call wouldn't connect. "If he hurts Jax . . ." His eyes flashed as his temper boiled to the surface. "He'll wish he'd never been born! We'll blitz him on social media, we'll hack into his accounts, we'll steal his identity! We'll prove that the keyboard is mightier than the sword!"

I clenched my fists. My eyes also filled with tears, but they were angry tears and they stung. "We have to call the police," I told Tyler. "We have to call Mom and Dad!"

"No." Pyrrha wrapped both her hands around Tyler's hand, which was still clutching the phone. "If you want Jax to be safe, you must do what I tell you." She looked beseechingly into his eyes. "Please, Tyler, please listen to me."

He went quiet all of a sudden. Pyrrha's elixir had made Tyler happy, but her voice seemed to work in a different way. "I'm listening."

"You and Ethan must deliver the urn of Love to Zeus. Immediately."

I felt like I'd been punched in the gut. "Huh?"

"Take my leather bag and go to the portal."

"You want us to . . . ?" I could barely speak. "But . . ."

"The bag is the key. Tell Poseidon you have the urn. He will allow you passage."

"Oh wow," Tyler said, his face going ghostly white. "Are you serious? We're going into the Realm of the Gods? I need to sit down." He leaned against the car. "I can't believe this is happening."

"No way!" I said. "We should call Homeland Security, or the National Guard, or . . ." But even as I said this, I knew it was futile. Ricardo could open the urn of Faith and turn an entire army into mindless followers in a matter of seconds.

"Listen to me, Ethan." Pyrrha gripped my shoulders. "My father is infected with madness. No one in your world can stop him. But he does not know that we have found the urn of Love, so there is still a chance for us to be successful. But in order for us to keep Jax safe and to get the urn of Faith, I must go to him. In the meantime, you must deliver Love to Zeus."

"But Jax?" I asked.

"I will protect her." She hugged me. Then she turned to Tyler. "This is what you have long dreamed about. You have prepared your whole life for this quest. Deliver Love and you will be my hero." She kissed his cheek.

I'd never seen that particular expression on my brother's face. He looked seasick and happy at the same time.

Then, before we could say another word, before I could offer one more reason why this was the craziest plan in the history of plans, she ran from the parking lot. That's when I saw the black limousine. It slowed for a moment, only long enough for Pyrrha to climb into the front passenger seat. I saw the brim of Ricardo's fedora. Without a wave or even a glance, Pyrrha closed the door. The limo drove away.

My heart sank. I could see the outline of a face pressed against the tinted back window. I couldn't see her expression, but I guessed she was scared.

I looked at the red urn. So small, so unobtrusive, yet capable of draining love from someone's soul. Love is an odd thing—sometimes you don't notice it until you're faced with losing it.

"Jax," I whispered.

We try to express love with words, with greeting cards and gifts. But the best way to express it is through action. I turned to Tyler. "What do we do now?"

Tyler snapped out of his daze. He pulled his car keys from his pocket and yanked open the driver's door. "We do what all heroes do before setting out on a quest. We assemble a team and then we go to battle."

28
TYLER

REPORT #572B, FILED BY: Tyler Hoche, Team Captain
MISSION: Quest to Return Urn of Love to Zeus,
Rescue Jax Malone from an Insane Criminal, and
Save the World!
TEAM MEMBERS: Ethan Hoche, Promoted from
Technical Officer to 2nd in Command

TIME: Now
LOCATION: Boston, MA

. . . to be continued.

Acknowledgments

Huge thanks to Phoebe Segal, PhD, who is the Mary Bryce Comstock Assistant Curator of Greek and Roman Art at the Museum of Fine Arts in Boston. She very nicely answered my questions about the facility and the marble head of Aphrodite, known as the Bartlett Head. If you go to the museum, be sure to look for this lovely piece of art, but do not attempt to steal it! It no longer contains the urn of Love.

Thanks also to Melissa Miller, Claudia Gabel, Katherine Tegen, and the entire team at Harper-Collins Publishers. I wrote this entire novel from my yacht, and they never complained about the waterlogged pages or the flecks of seagull poop.